Joyful Holiday
Seasons
by

Cynthia Moore

Joyful Holiday Seasons

Cover Art by *RJMorris*

The Wild Rose Press, Inc.
PO Box 708
Adams Basin, NY 14410-0708
Visit us at www.thewildrosepress.com

Publishing History
First Tea Rose Edition, 2017
Print ISBN 978-1-5092-1808-0

Published in the United States of America

Table of Contents

Gift of Love

by

Cynthia Moore

Dedication

This story is dedicated to my daughter, Emily, with love.

Prologue

December 20, 1815, Chesham County, England

Lady Rebecca Hastings, the daughter of the Earl and Countess of Winton, of Amersham, England pulled her black riding habit more closely around herself as the chill evening air crept inside the garment. She shivered and stared down at the gravestone thrusting up from the barren ground in front of her.

James Thompson Earl of Archly Chesham, England
A Brave Peer and Captain Who Met His Untimely Death
With Great Valor at the Battle of Waterloo
May He Rest In Peace
April 10, 1783—June 18, 1815

This was to have been her wedding day. She and James would have been together as man and wife at last. Rebecca hastily pulled off one of her riding gloves, reached inside a small pocket sewn in the side of her skirt, and pulled out a heart-shaped, white enameled locket framed in seed pearls. She studied the rough likeness of James on the front of the token for a few moments and then turned it over to examine the lock of hair covered in crystal on the reverse side. James had presented it to her just days before he'd left Chesham to join Wellington and his fellow officers in Brussels in late May.

A horse whinnied, and she looked up to see Jacob,

her groom, walking her mare and his horse briskly back and forth in an effort to keep them warm in the frigid December air.

Rebecca turned back to the locket that lay like a talisman across her palm. Carefully placing the keepsake on the frosty ground at her feet, she reached into her pocket once more for the small piece of mistletoe she had brought to adorn her sweetheart's grave.

With the sprig of greenery in her hand, she kneeled down in front of the gravestone.

"I love you, James. I miss you so much," Rebecca whispered softly as she bent over to place the piece of mistletoe on the grave.

A bead of moisture fell from her eye and moved down across her cheek. She came to her feet once more and hastily reached up to brush the tear away.

"Rebecca, I have come to speak with you."

She held herself absolutely still as the voice pierced her consciousness. It could not be! It could not be James' voice. It was very similar, but it sounded somewhat muffled, as if the person was speaking from a great distance away.

As she stood there listening for the voice once again, her gaze fell upon the locket on the ground at her feet. What she observed caused her eyes to widen in astonishment. The token was glowing brightly, almost as if it were on fire. Rebecca moved forward to touch it, but she abruptly halted as a sudden burst of icy, cold air caressed the side of her face.

"It is I, James. Do not be afraid, my dear. Please let me speak with you."

Rebecca stared at the gravestone once more and spoke haltingly, "James, James? Is it…truly you? How is this…possible?"

"The locket represents me in life. When you placed it upon my grave, it allowed my spirit, which is not at peace, to make itself known to you once more."

Rebecca covered her mouth with her hand and then looked hastily over her shoulder at Jacob who was still walking the horses on the other side of the gate to the cemetery.

"He cannot hear me, Rebecca. Only you are aware of my unearthly presence."

She slowly lowered her hand to her side as she continued to stare at the gleaming jewelry. "Wh-what, what do want to say to me, James?"

The locket shimmered even brighter for a moment and then Rebecca heard the hushed voice of the spirit once again. "I wish to remind you of your promise to me before I left you, my dear."

She attempted to calm her racing pulse and will her scattered thoughts to a semblance of order. She quickly gave up the struggle. Circumstances at this moment did not lend themselves to orderly reasoning. "Wh-what promise do you refer t-to James?"

"We spoke of my wish that you would not unduly mourn for me if I were killed in battle. You promised me you would not waste your life lamenting my loss. Yet, here it is over six months since my death and you still grieve. You sew samplers and embroider chair covers with only your companion or mother as company during the day. You don't attend any public activities, and you rarely shop for new garments. In fact, you scarcely leave the shelter of your parents' home."

Rebecca momentarily forgot her unease at conversing with a spirit as annoyance at James' unjust impressions caused her to answer him back with indignation. "Surely you realize that my promise was made to you with no real intention of ever being required to fulfill it? Although sweethearts, mothers and wives are well aware of the dangers of war, we must strive to keep thoughts of the possible deaths of our loved ones pushed back to the very farthest recesses of our minds in the interest of our own sanity."

"I understand that, my dear. But I did die. It is time for you to move on. Do not waste your life wishing for something that can never be. I must leave you soon, Rebecca." The spirit's voice suddenly became much softer. "Please visit me again tomorrow. And bring the locket with you."

Rebecca became conscious of the cold air briefly touching the side of her cheek once more, a hissing noise, and a slight movement from the locket as it lay on the hard ground. The piece of jewelry suddenly lost its glistening aura and became merely a token of remembrance again.

She swiftly reached for it and turned it over. Other than fleeting warmth on the surface, nothing had changed. Quickly dropping the token into her pocket, Rebecca moved to join her groom and then mount her horse for a swift canter home.

Chapter One

"You look like you've seen a ghost."

Rebecca abruptly turned. "Adrian, you're home!" she cried out as she flung herself into the outstretched arms of her childhood friend, Adrian Russell, Marquess of Burton. He was the older son of the Duke and Duchess of Haverston and grew up on the neighboring estate of Haverston Hall.

She eagerly studied her handsome friend. His thick, dark brown, slightly wavy hair was brushed back from his broad forehead. Deep blue eyes were framed by full, black lashes. A straight, aristocratic nose and full, firm lips completed his handsome visage. Rebecca noted with some concern that his skin color was slightly paler than normal, and his coat of dark blue superfine hung loosely across his chest underneath his cloak as if he had lost weight. She concluded that the rigors of war had greatly affected Adrian. No doubt he would brush any concerns that she might express over his health aside, opting instead to reassure her of his well-being once he had properly rested and filled his stomach with regular meals of hearty English fare.

Adrian had left his estate Burton Hall in Berkhamsted and joined James on his journey to Brussels in May. He'd been at James' side when a French soldier had fired his musket into James' heart during the Battle of Waterloo. Adrian had promptly draped James' lifeless body across the front of his own saddle and ridden through the climax of the battle, emerging unscathed. He'd delivered his grievous burden to the officers' residence in town. There he secured a lined box for the corpse and received permission to escort James' body back to England. Rebecca had not seen Adrian since the funeral because he had immediately returned to Brussels and rejoined his regiment.

Rebecca loosened her arms from around Adrian's neck. He stood very still looking down at her with a concerned expression. It was then she remembered his initial comment. "I have just returned from James' gravesite," she admitted, pensively. "Perhaps it was ill advised, but this was to have been our wedding day."

"I would never presume to tell you that a visit to James' grave was ill advised, Rebecca," Adrian answered somberly. "I know you both agreed to put off your wedding for a time when James was called to duty. A day as special as this was to be will certainly bring you cherished memories of your time together. I can readily understand your need to visit the churchyard."

"Thank you, Adrian. I've missed your counsel since you went away." She placed one gloved hand on his forearm. "Come, let's go inside. It is quite chilly standing out here on the steps. Please join us for tea."

Adrian grinned down at her. "Are you certain that I'm welcome? Your mother doesn't expect me."

Rebecca tugged on his cloak and drew him toward the entry for an answer. "My mother would never forgive me if I let you return home without allowing her to speak with you."

An elderly butler stood somewhat stiffly at the top

of the marble steps. This upstanding, dignified servant had been with the family for over forty years. His portly and ever cheerful wife had been their housekeeper for almost thirty years. He held the heavy oak door wide open to welcome them inside.

"Thank you so much, Cord," Rebecca called out to him as they reached the top step. "You remember Adrian Russell, the Marquess of Burton?"

The butler bowed and reached for Adrian's cloak, hat, and gloves. "Good afternoon, my lord. Of course I remember Lord Burton, my lady."

"Many a time we tried his patience didn't we, Lady Rebecca?" Adrian questioned after he had warmly greeted the longtime fixture of the household. "I remember we were seldom where we were supposed to be."

"Yes, but we didn't mean to cause him problems. I believe it was simply a matter of impatience on our part. We never seemed to stay in one place for very long."

Adrian looked at Cord who stood silently at their side. "I don't think he would agree with your assessment," he answered with a quizzical lift of one of his brows.

At that moment, a door off the main hallway opened. "Do I hear voices? My goodness, is that you, Adrian?" exclaimed Rebecca's mother, Lady Winton. She was still a very handsome woman, tall and slender. Her thick auburn hair only contained a few gray strands. She wore a simple, light green morning gown with a wool shawl draped across her shoulders for added warmth.

Lady Winton rushed out of the sitting room and clasped Adrian's outstretched hands. "My dear boy, it is wonderful that you have returned home safely. When did you arrive? How long will you stay? Oh, how I run on! Rebecca, please go and change out of your riding habit. Miss Frost and I will entertain our guest until you join us for tea. Come with me, Lord Burton."

Rebecca exchanged a bemused grin with Adrian as her mother propelled him toward the door to the sitting room. She turned to hurry up the staircase. Once inside her room, she rushed over to the wall to grab the bell pull and ring for her maid, Lily.

"I am here, my lady," Lily called out moments later as she opened the chamber door.

Rebecca was attempting to unfasten the remaining buttons on her jacket. She tossed the garment onto the back of a chair and then strode across the room to her dressing table. Carefully reaching inside the pocket on her skirt, she withdrew James' locket and wrapped it in a handkerchief. She lifted the lid of her jewelry box and placed the memento inside, closing the lid securely. She twisted around to face her maid. "I need to change for tea. Quickly now, Lord Burton has returned and is even now conversing with my mother and Miss Frost in the sitting room."

Lily paused in front of the wardrobe to turn with a look of surprise. "Lord Burton is here, my lady?"

"Yes, he is. I've only had a moment to converse with him. I know nothing whatsoever of his reasons for returning or of his plans for the future."

With raised eyebrows, Lily turned back to study her mistress's various garments. "Will the violet day dress be appropriate, my lady?"

"Yes, that is perfect." Rebecca dropped her gloves onto the bed, and her maid helped her change her clothes.

A short time later, Rebecca emerged from her bedchamber gracefully attired in the violet gown with a Norwich shawl wrapped across her shoulders to ward off any chill in the drafty rooms. Her long, auburn hair had been vigorously brushed until the red highlights shone brightly like hot coals in a fire. The tresses were caught up with a tortoiseshell comb in a loose bun at the crown of her head. Wispy tendrils escaped from the fastening to curl softly across the back of her neck. Her green eyes glowed reflecting her excitement.

She nodded her thanks as Cord arrived outside the sitting room just before her. He opened the door and announced Rebecca before bowing and allowing her to pass.

"Ah, you look much more suitable, my dear. I always liked that gown. Violet normally would not suit your hair color, but the fabric is a shade that complements and does not detract. Come sit beside Miss Frost." Lady Winton indicated the empty spot next to Rebecca's companion on the settee.

Miss Frost looked up from the embroidery she had been diligently working on and pushed her spectacles farther up the bridge of her nose. The lady's thin frame was covered by two shawls, and a heavy blanket rested across her lap. "Good evening, my lady. Your cheeks look slightly flushed. I trust that your ride to the churchyard did not cause you to catch a chill?" Miss Frost's slight build made her imagine herself to be quite frail, and she frequently worried about the state of other people's health.

"I'm fine. Perhaps my skin is slightly reddened as a result of the elation I'm feeling to have Lord Burton back in our country seat once again."

Adrian, who had come to his feet as she'd entered the room, sat down once more on the chair to her left. "Thank you very much for your gracious words, Rebecca. Your gown is lovely. I was just telling your mother that I have sold my commission. I'm going to reside at Haverston Hall for the foreseeable future."

Rebecca turned to him with a look of surprise. "Thank you so much for the compliment. But I don't understand why you would not wish to return to your own estate."

Adrian took a deep breath before he answered her statement. "I received a letter from my mother over a month ago. She expressed concern over the state of my father's health. Initially it was nothing very serious. But now, he's had several bouts of memory loss in the last year. Most recently his steward reported to my mother that my father had failed to keep several previously set engagements with other business partners and friends. He also forgot to show up for an appointment with his tailor in London last month."

"My goodness, your mother certainly had reason to be worried. She was right to contact you," exclaimed Lady Winton.

"Now that I've been home several days, I'm glad that she voiced her concerns to me. Although my father seems relatively unchanged as he performs his normal daily tasks, anything unusual or out of the way is simply forgotten."

"Does your father appear distracted in any way?" Rebecca asked anxiously.

"Nothing out of the ordinary for a peer who owns a large estate and has many responsibilities," Adrian assured her. "My mother and I have consulted with his doctor and thankfully he said that blood-letting would produce no benefits. He believes the memory loss is simply a foreshadowing of old age. As you are probably aware, my father is twenty years older than my mother."

He paused and stared into the fire before continuing, "With Napoleon safely installed on St. Helena, my usefulness as an officer in the British Life Guards is currently at a minimum. When I received the news of my father's affliction, it seemed best to sell out at this time and assist with the management of Haverston Hall."

A discreet knock sounded on the door, and Cord entered with a flourish announcing the imminent arrival of the tea tray.

"Rebecca, please do the honors and pour for us," instructed her mother. "I will pass around Mrs. Teakle's luscious apple tarts."

Lady Winton waited to speak until everyone was served. She took a drink of her tea and then turned toward their guest. "Is your father aware of his loss of memory?"

"He's certainly aware that appointments have been missed. But he's a proud man and frankly the situation is delicate." Adrian paused to take a sip of the hot liquid. "He assumes he was not told or reminded of the engagements. I will take care that my assistance with the management of the estate appears minimal to him when in reality I plan on taking more and more control of the daily operations. My mother and I will also do our best to interact as normally as possible with him and not to berate him in any way for his infirmity."

"Is Paul aware of your father's affliction?" asked

Rebecca.

He nodded before speaking. "My brother arrives here tomorrow on holiday from his studies at Cambridge. I have written and advised him of the situation. I received a brief note in reply from him this morning. He is naturally dismayed to hear the news but agrees with our decision to treat father as if nothing had changed."

He lowered his empty plate to set it on a nearby table. "Before I speak any further on this subject, I must extend an invitation from my mother. She wishes for you, Lady Winton and Lord Winton, Lady Rebecca and Miss Frost, to join my family for a Christmas holiday celebration dinner two evenings from today."

Before a reply could be uttered, the sitting room door was thrust open. An older gentleman with sparse gray hair entered the chamber. It was the Earl of Winton himself. He was slightly taller than his spouse with a commanding presence, especially in close quarters. At present, he was dressed casually in buff-colored breeches, topped with a linen shirt, an informally tied cravat, and a dark green woolen waistcoat over which he wore a frock coat. "Do not fret, Cord. I can announce myself. Ah, it appears that I am only slightly tardy for tea."

"My dear, see who has joined us! Lord Burton has returned home at last!" Lady Winton proclaimed as she indicated an empty chair for her husband's use directly across from his daughter's seat.

Lord Winton turned away from his wife to greet his neighbor's older son with genuine pleasure. He strode across the room and clapped Adrian upon the back as that gentleman stood up and lowered his head slightly in deference to the earl.

"Lord Burton! It's wonderful to have you back, young man! But when did you arrive? Your father sent us no news." Lord Winton stopped speaking and looked somewhat perplexed. "In fact I have heard very little from your sire of late. Is everything well at Haverston Hall?"

Adrian shook his head. "I regret to inform you, my lord, that my father has recently suffered several serious lapses in memory. It is for that very reason my mother contacted me and requested my presence here in Amersham."

Lord Winton drew his eyebrows lower over his eyes and studied Adrian intently. "How long has your father's memory loss been evident?"

"We believe it started a few months ago. Fortunately, his health has not otherwise been adversely affected in any way."

A clock struck the hour in the hall.

"I must ask you to excuse me, Lord Winton, Lady Winton, Lady Rebecca, and Miss Frost. I need to return to Haverston Hall. May I tell my mother that you will all attend the celebration?"

"Yes, of course. I'll provide my husband with the other details of your father's illness. Please tell the duchess that we will gladly attend her gathering. I look forward to visiting with your parents and your brother as well."

"I expect a more detailed account of your recent activities in the British Life Guards at a later time, young man," forewarned Lord Winton.

"I'll ring for your horse to be brought around, Adrian," Rebecca offered as she stood up and crossed the room to the bell pull.

Cord answered Rebecca's summons promptly. She delivered her request for Adrian's horse. The butler moved to do her bidding only to turn around once more as the countess hailed him.

"Please ensure that all is in readiness for the delivery of the Yule log tomorrow morning."

Lord Winton added, "I instructed the lads this morning as to its location, my dear. They'll collect it soon after dawn. We should have it here a few hours later."

"Excellent." Lady Winton heard this news with pleasure. She turned toward her daughter. "We'll decorate the rooms with greenery tomorrow shortly after breaking our fast."

Cord left to issue instructions. Miss Frost suddenly stood up, clasping her two shawls around her bony shoulders. She reached down awkwardly and endeavored to fold the blanket that had been resting across her lap. Quickly giving up on her attempt at neatness, she dropped the blanket into a jumbled heap onto a nearby empty stool. Then she gathered her embroidery and set it in a basket at her feet. "If you will excuse me, Lord and Lady Winton, Lady Rebecca and Lord Burton, I informed Mrs. Cord that I would assist Mrs. Teakle with the wrapping of the sweetmeats, almonds, and raisins in paper for the children on the estate, so they would be ready to place with the greenery tomorrow."

"Certainly you are excused, Miss Frost. I know they would greatly appreciate your assistance." She exited the room and Rebecca moved to stand next to Adrian as her parents tendered their goodbyes to him.

"I will leave you to your holiday preparations, Lord and Lady Winton." Adrian bowed to the couple. "Will you accompany me to the door, Lady Rebecca?" he asked her with a trace of the warm smile that she remembered so well.

"It would be my pleasure." She turned back toward her parents. "I'll rejoin you both momentarily."

Rebecca paused in front of the sitting room door as Adrian reached around her to pull it open. They left together and strolled down the main corridor toward the entrance.

He suddenly increased his pace and stepped in front of Rebecca causing her to abruptly come to a standstill. She looked up at her companion with a questioning expression on her face.

"It appears that you enjoy riding in the chill December climate. Will you join me for an early morning canter tomorrow?"

Rebecca immediately began pondering how best to agree to Adrian's plan as well as accomplishing her visit to the churchyard.

He seemed to have mistaken her initial hesitation for reluctance. "I realize I materialized quite unexpectedly on your doorstep today. Certainly you must be quite occupied with holiday matters…"

Rebecca reached out and lightly squeezed Adrian's forearm before quickly releasing him. "You don't understand. I wish to go riding with you, but I need to make a visit somewhere else before I meet with you. I was deliberating how best to accomplish both obligations."

Adrian placed his hand on her shoulder and gazed intently into her green eyes. "Will you tell me where else you propose to go? Perhaps I can join you."

She stared down at the thick hall carpet under her feet. "I planned to visit James' grave once again in the morning."

Adrian released Rebecca's arm and cupped her chin. He applied gentle pressure until she raised her head to meet his direct gaze with a slightly sheepish look of her own. "I meant what I said to you earlier. I would never berate you for visiting James' grave."

Rebecca sighed with relief and smiled at Adrian. He gently rubbed the soft skin on the edge of her jaw before lowering his hand. She was disconcerted to feel a prick of moisture upon her eyelashes. She hastily reached up to pat her eyes with her fingers before answering. "You are very understanding. I assure you that I have not spent my days since the funeral languishing at his graveside. But the Christmas holidays seem to have brought his presence and spirit back to me in full force." In more ways than you can know, she thought to herself.

"Perhaps you will permit me to join you shortly after you plan to arrive at the churchyard? We could go for a short ride through the park if you do not think it would be too cold for such activity."

"Of course, I would enjoy that. Contrary to what Miss Frost believes, I rarely become chilled when I am outside in winter."

"It must be the remnants of your hoydenish ways from when you were a girl. You were rarely at a standstill. You definitely kept warm with your constant pranks and rollicking escapades in those days."

She giggled as his words brought back somewhat embarrassing memories of their mischief-making. "I seem to remember that you and Paul were up to plenty of antics yourselves."

Adrian looked back at her in mock consternation. "I can see I will need to refresh your memories of what transpired during our ride tomorrow, Becky."

Rebecca's smiling visage became serious when he used his pet name for her from their youth. "It's been a long time since I've been called that."

"Since I was the only person who gave you that nickname, certainly it was I who last said it. You must have done something very outrageous to deserve the designation." he teased her as he started to walk toward the front door. "I will meet you at the churchyard about eight o'clock tomorrow morning."

"You always did treat me like a sister."

Adrian stopped and turned back to her with an arrested expression. He looked intently at Rebecca before saying, "Conclusions are sometimes reached without the use of common sense."

With that cryptic comment, he turned to collect his cloak, hat, and gloves from Cord. He strode out of the door without a backward glance leaving Rebecca standing alone in the hallway attempting to comprehend Adrian's parting words.

Chapter Two

"It doesn't seem quite as cold this morning, Jacob. I shouldn't be too long." Rebecca handed her groom the reins. "Perhaps you can discover a patch of grass somewhere close by."

"Don't ye concern yourself, my lady. I will keep your mare warm."

Rebecca nodded her thanks and turned to open the ornate iron gate that led to the churchyard. She walked toward James' grave being watchful in case anything out of the ordinary should happen.

Just as she had done the previous day, Rebecca stood and stared down at the headstone before reaching into the pocket of her riding habit and pulling out the locket.

The trinket was still securely wrapped in her handkerchief. She carefully removed the fabric to reveal James' profile on the front of the locket. She studied his image for a moment before she bent over and placed the token on the ground quite near the spot it had been resting on the day before.

"Oh, my goodness!" She had scarcely removed her hand from the locket when it began to shine brightly. Rebecca stumbled backward, and her body began to shake, shocked anew by the uncanny phenomenon she was witnessing.

The cold burst of air once again caressed her cheek.

Rebecca squeezed her eyes shut and clasped her gloved hands tightly. She willed herself to stand tall and stiff as a soldier as she waited for the next episode to play out.

"Good of you to visit me once again, Rebecca."

James' voice sounded weakly in her ears. "J-James, is there some way to reassure myself that I'm not dreaming this? If I'm truly not in some kind of a trance, could you explain to me how this happens?" She raised her tightly gripped hands over her head in a pleading gesture. "Have pity on me, I'm a mere mortal. You were killed at Waterloo last June. How can you be here speaking to me now?"

The bare branches of the trees which circled the churchyard made popping and cracking sounds as a sudden wind swirled through them. The loud noises caused Rebecca to open her eyes. She lowered her arms to her sides and studied the locket as it continued to glow brightly upon the chilled ground.

"I'm unable to offer you any proof other than the evidence in your own heart," the ghostly voice answered. "You promised me you would not mourn for me. Oh, yes, you present a calm, content façade to the people you come in contact with each day. You believe that's enough to satisfy those who care for you and love you. But you're wrong, Rebecca. They know you have changed. You've lost your sparkle and fervor. Yes, we loved each other, we planned to marry, and I was killed in war. It is right to mourn me for a time.

"The problem occurred when you made a vow to me the last time we spoke. You promised not to waste your life lamenting my loss. You have not kept that pledge. For that reason, my spirit has not been at rest. When you placed the locket on my grave, it allowed my spirit to be released and to make myself known to you. I can't tell you any more than that."

"Thank you for your explanation, James. Perhaps I will never truly understand how this has happened but your reasons have helped me to face the situation more calmly." She raised her head and looked forward, not really seeing anything. "From what you've told me, I gather that your spirit is restless and you wish to be at peace. I believe somehow I am to play a part in restoring your serenity. How am I to do this? You know I wish you nothing but tranquility and repose in your afterlife." The strands of hair that had escaped from underneath her hat brushed against her neck as the cool air surrounded her once again.

"Therein lays the problem. My spirit can never be truly at peace if I tell you what needs to be accomplished. You must come to the conclusion without prompting from me. I can only ask that you let go of the pall of grief which still hangs over you. Expose the shadow that covers your deeper emotions. Allow your heart to beat freely once more."

Rebecca knelt and put one gloved hand on the gravestone. "I will attempt to do as you ask, James. I hadn't realized that I am distressing my family and friends."

"Thank you. I'm certain you will once again find true happiness. Please return here on Christmas Eve morning. My otherworldly sense tells me that you may have something important to tell me then."

The iron gate clicked as it was opened.

"Am I disturbing you?" Adrian inquired softly as he approached the gravesite carrying a small bouquet of red roses.

Rebecca looked up in surprise and then swiftly glanced behind her. Nothing out of the ordinary was visible. She hastily shifted her stance and covered the gleaming locket with the bottom edge of her skirt. "No, no, please join me. Where did you obtain the beautiful roses at this time of year?"

"My mother had a greenhouse built last spring. She has worked tirelessly with our gardener George Small. She's enjoying the novelty of having roses in the house during the wintertime, too." He moved past Rebecca and carefully placed the roses at the foot of James' headstone.

As he bent over, Rebecca reached down to retrieve the locket. When Adrian stood up once again, he glanced at her hand as she dropped the token into the pocket of her skirt. "Is that the memento James gave you before we left to join our regiments? May I see it?"

Rebecca felt her face flush slightly as she realized Adrian had spotted her furtive movement. "Of course," she quickly assured him as she pulled the locket back out of her skirt.

He studied James' likeness on the front of the token before turning it over in his palm to look at the lock of hair encased in the back. Then he reached out and placed the item back onto her gloved palm. He did not remove his hand. The locket rested warmly between their clasped hands. "I never said much about what occurred at Waterloo to you at James' funeral. My time here was very brief and you were clearly too upset to listen to many details."

"Yes, that day was an unhappy one for all of us."

"I want to assure you that James felt no pain when he was killed. We were charging forward and our flank became mired in the thick mud and fell back. James and I were exposed momentarily, and a bullet from a French cuirassier's gun struck him directly in his heart. He died instantly."

Rebecca stared down at their clasped hands. As she listened to Adrian's description of the battle, her heart began to feel heavy, a brick inside her chest. She could picture James as he valiantly pushed his horse forward into the center of the battlefield, not knowing that in the next moment his life would end forever.

She looked up at her companion studying her with concern and knew instantly that Adrian's presence at her side was playing an important role in her recovery from James' death. As they continued to stand with their hands clasped together around the locket, Rebecca became conscious of a subtle feeling of relief. The pain was still present, but now it was softened by the knowledge she'd just gained. "I'm glad you told me. I must admit that I felt very sad when I first heard your description of the battle. But now that I know James didn't feel any pain when he died, I feel very relieved and comforted."

"Perhaps now you can break free of the deep sorrow that I fear has dominated your life since you were told of James' passing and you can begin to face each day with a lighter heart."

A whinnying came from the adjacent field. Adrian lightly squeezed Rebecca's hand before releasing it and reaching out to gently bend her fingers to cover the locket. "Put that away safely. Are you ready to take a short ride now? It appears the horses are becoming restless."

Rebecca hastily wrapped the trinket back in her

handkerchief and tucked it securely away in her skirt pocket once more. With a slight nod toward Adrian, she indicated she was ready to leave. They walked briskly toward Jacob who was patiently tramping back and forth across the gravel roadway with all three horses in tow.

"Well done," Adrian greeted the groom with praise. "Hand me the reins to Lady Rebecca's mare."

He led her mare to one side and then assisted her to mount. Once she was seated in the sidesaddle, Adrian mounted his own horse. Jacob was left to follow behind them.

They gave their horses their heads and allowed them to canter through the open fields. When they reached the meadow, they slowed their horses to a walk. Jacob followed at a discreet distance.

Adrian guided his horse closer to her side. "I was thinking about what we were discussing with Cord yesterday. We were certainly mischief-makers when we were growing up. Do you remember when we would accompany your governess, Miss Spotter, bring a picnic here, quickly devour most of the food, and then meander through the wood looking for old coins?"

Rebecca giggled. "Oh, yes, I remember searching and searching for those coins. Miss Spotter was quite beside herself attempting to keep us in sight. Paul had read somewhere that King James the first had passed through this area on the way to London at one time. We were certain we would eventually discover some sort of treasure."

"We didn't ever find anything valuable, did we?"

Rebecca pondered his query as her mare ambled along frequently lowering her head to sniff at the frozen undergrowth. "I found a coin that was not old, and I remember that Paul unearthed a piece of broken pottery. I don't remember you finding anything of interest at all."

"I was probably too focused on assisting you in your searches to explore on my own," Adrian replied with a grin.

Rebecca turned to study him for a moment and then spoke. "The three of us certainly spent many hours together plotting new schemes. Paul and I were lost when you left to go to Cambridge."

"I thought you two were still able to come up with some sort of diversions after I had departed."

"Oh, yes we managed to invent a few escapades that kept us entertained for a time." Rebecca stared across the open meadow to the stand of barren walnut trees that ringed the edge of the park. "Then I began to spend more and more time on my own in the summerhouse."

"What did you find to occupy you there?"

Rebecca blushed rosily as she contemplated Adrian's question. She turned to face him. "I spent most of my time there dreaming of meeting a handsome gentleman, falling in love, and getting married. You must know, daydreaming is one of the silly things young girls do in their free time," she ended, a touch defiantly.

"I confess, I find it hard to imagine the little miss, who acted like a hoyden for most of the time I spent with her, would suddenly change and spend her days by herself mooning over an imaginary person," he countered.

"I knew you would find it hard to relate the girl you knew when you went away, to the woman I became soon after," Rebecca answered, somewhat soberly. "And then, almost four years later, I met James."

"I had forgotten. How did you meet?"

"James had heard of my father's interest in crop rotation; that we were experimenting with its methods. He visited Winton Woods to observe the process."

She reached out to pat her mare's neck before continuing. "Cord informed James that my father was out in the fields and told him how to reach him. I was returning home from gathering flowers on the southern edge of our property when I nearly collided with James and his horse on the pathway."

"That was just before I graduated from Cambridge."

"Yes, you returned about a fortnight later. By that time, James was a frequent visitor to Winton Woods. In fact, I believe you met him the evening you arrived back home," she remembered with some surprise.

"I was intent on informing you that I had come back. I was loath to wait another day. I hopped onto my horse and rode like the wind, disregarding my family's advice to wait to visit you until morning," he replied somewhat ruefully.

"It is all coming back to me!" Rebecca exclaimed, her eyes widening in surprise as she remembered. "James had asked my father's permission to pay his addresses to me that very evening. We were in the sitting room celebrating when you were announced."

"I was so eager to see you that I barely noticed the other occupants in the room. I rushed up to you and grabbed your hands only to realize that a tall, muscular gentleman was standing at your side observing my actions with some confusion." Adrian abruptly stopped speaking and studied Rebecca's expression intently.

She gripped the reins tightly as more details of the evening came rushing back. "I was so surprised when you walked into the room. In the excitement and confusion caused by your sudden appearance, I momentarily forgot that you and James had never met. I was embarrassed when you abruptly stepped away from me and James inquired, somewhat bluntly, if he could be formally presented."

"That was certainly a very awkward moment," Adrian agreed. He sat up straight and stiff in the saddle. "However, the oversight was swiftly remedied by your father, he introduced me and we moved on."

"Yes, you became fast friends. Then James and I agreed to postpone our wedding when it appeared that Napoleon would never be brought to heel. You both went off to join your regiments soon after." Rebecca suddenly recalled an occasion when she had interrupted a heated discussion between the two men. "The age difference between you never caused any tension or resentment in the beginning?" Rebecca inquired. She steadied her mare as it side-stepped over to the edge of the path.

"At first things were a little awkward. James was only three years older than I am, but he seemed to feel that he needed to play the role of mentor and advisor with me. I was forced to make it clear to him a few times quite early on in our acquaintance that I was perfectly able to make my own decisions. Once James realized that I was uncomfortable with his somewhat domineering attitude, he stopped all attempts to control my life and we became close companions," Adrian explained. He pulled back on the reins and reached down to pat the mane of his horse as it pranced forward.

"I know James was very impressed with your accomplishments the day we visited your estate in

Berkhamsted. Burton Keep is so well maintained, Adrian. I remember the grounds were so lush and green. The house was so welcoming and warm inside. You must feel slightly disenchanted at your inability to return to your home at present," Rebecca said with some concern.

Adrian smiled down upon her before answering. "I admit that I miss my home. But as you know, my parents urgently required my assistance at Haverston Hall. And it is Christmastime after all. My brother arrives later this afternoon. What better time to reside here with my family and my friends close by?"

Rebecca agreed with his observation before she noted Jacob's lone figure perched upon his horse behind them. "I promised Mother I would assist her with decorating the house. I should return home now."

"Of course. I will ride back with you as far as the Hall."

They guided their horses back around the edge of the meadow to join Jacob. Adrian spoke once again as they reached the pathway.

"Do you still spend time in the summerhouse, Rebecca?"

"I haven't been there since the day after James' funeral," she answered soberly. "As I explained to you, it was always a place for me to go to think and dream. As I grew older, I found myself going there when I needed to reflect upon a turning point in my life. I went there when James first asked my father for permission to pay his addresses to me and when you and James left to join your regiments. I suppose you could describe the episodes that I went to contemplate as life-altering situations."

"It sounds to me as if the secluded spot has played an important role in your life."

"Yes, it certainly has been influential in allowing me to sort my thoughts and emotions in privacy. My father never could have conceived that the house would be used for that purpose when he first had it constructed." She chuckled softly. "He initially built it for my mother as a place to escape from the main house to write her letters or to read. But she claims whenever she thinks of using it, the weather is too cool or rainy, and she hesitates to leave the relative warmth of the sitting room in that circumstance."

She decided not to ask him about the puzzling comment he had made to her the previous evening about conclusions and common sense. He might be vexed with her if he was required to explain himself. Soon the three riders arrived at the main gate to Haverston Hall. Adrian turned slightly in his saddle and saluted Rebecca with his riding crop. "I'll see you and your family here tomorrow evening for our holiday celebration dinner?"

"Yes, of course. We look forward to the occasion." She smiled warmly at her friend and lifted her gloved hand in farewell before guiding her mare forward with Jacob following close behind.

Chapter Three

Lady Winton, Miss Frost, and Rebecca moved to the drawing room immediately after breaking their fast. A housemaid joined them to assist with unwrapping ornaments that were placed among the greenery. One footman also stood by with a ladder to help hang the mistletoe.

Lady Winton handed several tiny wax tapers to Henry the footman. "Secure these candles to the leaves over the fireplace mantel."

"Yes, my lady," Henry replied as he sprinted up the ladder holding the tapers in his free hand.

Miss Frost lifted a small, gaily decorated chest in bright green and red from off the floor and deposited it on the table in front of Rebecca, trailing her shawls behind her. "Inside are the little wax dolls that you like to place among the greenery. Mrs. Cord told me she put them in this chest, which she discovered empty in the attic after the other crate broke apart."

"Thank you. Perhaps Sally can assist you with arranging the sweetmeat and almond papers." Rebecca indicated the young housemaid standing shyly in the corner of the room close to the door. She looked down at the chest and uttered an exclamation of surprise. "Mother, look at this."

As Miss Frost approached Sally and began to assemble the various fruits and nuts in wrappers for the estate children, Rebecca picked up the small container and brought it closer to her mother. Lady Winton studied the brightly colored item intently. "Is that not the chest that you made when you were about thirteen or fourteen years old?"

"Yes, it is. I thought it had been lost years ago." Rebecca gingerly placed the little chest on the floor and opened the lid. She reached inside and pulled out a wax angel carefully wrapped in a piece of white muslin. There were nine more similarly bundled angels in the box. When she had removed all the figures, Rebecca noticed that a tiny piece of the crate lining was lifted slightly in one corner. She reached inside in an attempt to fold the material back in place. Her fingers located something wedged underneath. The diminutive object came loose with a slight tug. She inspected the item and then began to giggle. "Mother, look what I have discovered. I had forgotten all about this. It is a tiny carved tree made from oak. Adrian made it for me about the time I made this chest." She held the object up for her mother to hold.

Lady Winton studied the little tree intently. "It has an inscription on it, '*To Becky. With Love, Adrian,*'" she read out loud. "How wonderful that you found this, my dear. It is a very special keepsake."

Her mother carefully dropped the carving back into Rebecca's outstretched hand. She wrapped it in a discarded piece of muslin and placed it upon the table in front of her. "I shall bring the little tree to the party tomorrow night. I doubt if Adrian remembers making it for me."

"Somehow I do not believe he has forgotten it, my dear."

Miss Frost interrupted their discussion. "Excuse me, we have finished arranging the children's gifts. Do they meet with your approval?"

Rebecca looked up at the decorations and smiled appreciatively. "Everything is quite lovely. Do you agree, Mother?"

"Oh, yes. I believe we have a much better display than last year. Sally and Henry can finish placing the last of the greenery on the end tables and then we will be finished."

Rebecca turned toward her companion. "Miss Frost, I have a few more gifts to purchase in town. Could you please accompany me for some last-minute Christmas shopping?"

"Of course, I can be ready in a few minutes."

"I will request the carriage to be brought around. Mother, do you need anything from town?"

"No, thank you, my dear, I have purchased everything I need."

"We will return in time for tea. Miss Frost, I will meet you downstairs in fifteen minutes."

"I will be ready, Lady Rebecca."

They entered the coach twenty minutes later. Once they were settled inside the vehicle with warm bricks at their feet and an extra shawl upon Miss Frost's lap, John Coachman gave the order for the horses to start.

Rebecca studied the barren, wintry landscape passing by. She thought of the upcoming celebrations and of the holiday party at Haverston Hall tomorrow evening. Another year was almost over, she thought with a sigh.

"Are you missing Lord Archly?" asked Miss Frost with concern when she heard her mistress's distressed murmur.

"Oh, my goodness!" Rebecca turned with a startled expression to her companion and then moved her gloved hands up to her face in an agitated manner to attempt to cover her suddenly flushed cheeks.

"Whatever is wrong? Do we need to order John Coachman to turn the coach around?" Miss Frost exclaimed, now quite distressed.

"I've just realized that I had not thought of James, Lord Archly for several hours. I feel quite guilty for not being true to his memory," Rebecca gasped fretfully.

Miss Frost reached across the coach to rest her gloved hand upon her charge's forearm. "I would never presume to advise you on how long it is proper to mourn for a man who you loved dearly and had planned to marry. However, I've been concerned at your continued low and downcast disposition. Today you were more like your old self, more content and at ease. I have also seen the elusive sparkle back in your eyes which had been missing since Lord Archly's death."

Rebecca listened intently to her companion while attempting to calm her jittery pulse. "You're not the first to mention my recurring somber disposition. I have lately agreed to rejoice in the part of James' life that I was lucky enough to share with him and not to perpetually lament his loss."

"I believe that is a very wise course to take. Not only for your own health and well-being but as a respite from the worry and concern your friends and family have experienced because of your continued gloomy and depressed temperament for the past few months. It is understandable to be sorrowful in the beginning, but now it is time to move on."

"I will do all I can to become more like the person I was before James' death," Rebecca vowed.

The coach rolled to a stop. Miss Frost began to gather her shawls together. Rebecca took several deep breaths in an effort to calm herself. The groom opened the door, bowed to the women, and lowered the step. After he assisted her and her companion to the ground, Rebecca stepped around to the front of the vehicle to give her orders to the driver.

"John, please meet us back here in just under an hour. We should have completed our errands by that time," she requested, feeling more like herself once again.

"I will do that, Lady Rebecca," replied John Coachman with a bow. He waited until the groom had taken his place beside him on the seat once more. Then he called out to the horses, and the coach rolled away.

Rebecca shook out her slightly crushed skirts while Miss Frost adjusted her shawls. Along the main avenue of the town, the walkways were teeming with people. It appeared that half of the population of Amersham had decided to do some last-minute Christmas shopping.

Rebecca strode forward calling out greetings and happy wishes of the season to acquaintances as she went along. Miss Frost managed to squirm past portly gentlemen, dodge boisterous groups of children attended by exhausted looking governesses, and stay relatively close to her charge's side.

Several people, both men and women, were intently studying the merchandise in the display windows of Douglas & Son Jewelry Store. Rebecca did not pause but proceeded inside.

The interior of the shop was also crowded with

customers. The elder, Mr. John Douglas, was behind the counter calling out an order to one of his clerks. "Lord Burton requested the necklace to be delivered to Haverston Hall tomorrow, Jack. See that it is done, lad."

"Yes, sir!" promised the harried clerk.

Rebecca raised her eyebrows slightly and shared a look of amusement with Miss Frost. "It appears that Lord Burton has been here before us. He has certainly wasted no time carrying out his Christmas purchases."

A bustling man who was a younger version of his father, John, halted in front of her and hastily bowed. "Good afternoon, Lady Rebecca. What items may I bring out for your perusal? Perhaps a coral necklace?"

"Thank you, but no, Mr. Douglas. I would like to purchase some earrings for my mother. May I please see your selection?"

"Of course. We have some particularly fine pieces that I could show you with tiny seed pearls and diamonds fashioned in delicate flowers surrounded and lined with silver."

Young Mr. Douglas brought out a tray with several delicately fashioned pairs of earrings. Rebecca studied them, discussed various merits with Miss Frost and finally decided upon a pair that included stems and leaves. The earrings were slightly larger than the other versions and they both agreed that Lady Winton would appreciate the jewelry's intricate design.

As the earrings were being wrapped, Rebecca studied some paintings of local landscapes displayed on the shop's rear walls. "Mr. Douglas, I don't remember noticing the paintings you have for sale at the back of the shop. Are they a new acquisition?"

"Why, yes, they are recently acquired. Widow

Barnes apparently has been painting local landscapes for several years. My father assisted the lady about a fortnight ago when she wanted an old table brought downstairs from her attic. Father discovered a treasure trove of paintings tucked away under an old blanket. He offered to sell some of the landscapes in our shop as a supplement to Mrs. Barnes' income."

Rebecca walked to the back of the shop to study the paintings. Miss Frost trailed close behind.

"There are the stand of trees and the meadow. This is the park where Lord Burton, Lord Paul Russell, and I spent so many happy days of our childhood!" she explained excitedly.

"It appears to be a very good representation of the area."

"Indeed it is," inserted Mr. Douglas, "we've had much interest in that particular painting. Lord Burton himself was examining it quite intently not too long ago this very morning."

"Of course!" exclaimed Rebecca as she thought over the clerk's words, "I must purchase this painting as a Christmas gift for him. The piece would have special meaning as well."

Both items were carefully wrapped and the payment was made. Rebecca and Miss Frost exited the shop a short time later, the former lady being extremely satisfied with her purchases.

****

The following evening found Rebecca examining her wardrobe apprehensively. Lily stood at her mistress' side patiently waiting for her to make a decision.

Rebecca sighed and pulled out a short-sleeved evening dress. A light green satin slip lay underneath a

British net frock. The sleeves on the garment were decorated with knots of green ribbon. The low-cut neckline was complemented by another piece of green ribbon placed directly underneath the bust. The skirt had a deep flounce ornamented with green holly leaves and red berries. "I suppose this dress aptly lends itself to a Christmas celebration," she commented resignedly.

"A wonderful choice, my lady. The light green color of the gown makes your auburn hair shine like gold."

"I must admit that your words create a glorious image." Rebecca suddenly felt much more enthusiastic about her selection, as she allowed her maid to draw the gown over her head. "Please remind me to bring the carved tree that Lord Burton made for me when we were children, to the dinner party."

A short time later with the tiny carving tucked securely in her reticule, Rebecca emerged from her bedchamber and descended the staircase to join Miss Frost, and her mother and father who were already gathered in the entryway.

"You look quite beautiful, my dear, as well as festive," complimented Lady Winton, who wore a silk evening dress in rich gold with a matching turban upon her head.

"No one would mistake the occasion," teased her father, who looked very handsome in his black, double-breasted cutaway frock coat, tan breeches, stockings, and black pumps. He carried a heavy wool cloak and a beaver hat in his hand.

"That shade of green is perfect on you, Lady Rebecca," added Miss Frost as she secured the top buttons on her black, woolen pelisse.

The two other women collected their fur-lined pelisses from Cord and then all four exited together.

The occupants of the coach spent their time discussing plans for Christmas. Just as Rebecca was assuring her mother of the fulfillment of her errands in town, John Coachman could be heard ordering the horses to stop. A moment later a footman outfitted in Haverston Hall livery was opening the door, bowing, and assisting them to alight.

Haverston Hall's butler, Jennings, met them at the top of the marble stairs. After bowing formally to Lord Winton and his party, he led them inside to a warm and festively decorated entry. Instructing a waiting footman to gather their gloves, hats and coats, he indicated that they should follow him to the formal drawing room. Jennings opened the door with a flourish.

"The Earl and Countess of Winton, Lady Rebecca Hastings and Miss Frost," he announced with another bow in the direction of the chamber.

Their party was greeted enthusiastically by the room's occupants. The Duchess of Haverston came forward and quickly embraced Lady Winton. The duchess was a few inches shorter and somewhat broader than the countess, but her hair was still the deep brown color of her youth and her complexion was quite smooth showing few wrinkles. She was dressed in a short-sleeved, red satin evening gown which was trimmed with a flounce of Chinchilla fur.

Lord Paul Russell assisted the duke out of his chair. Outwardly Lord Haverston appeared in good health although slightly frail. He wore clothing quite similar to Lord Winton, cutaway frock coat in dark blue, tan breeches and stockings and black pumps. They both greeted Lord and Lady Winton and Miss Frost. Then the duke reached for and held Rebecca's hand for a moment while gazing into her eyes with a blank expression in his own without speaking. Presently, he turned away, clasped his wife's shoulder, and engaged Lord and Lady Winton and Miss Frost in conversation. Rebecca stared at the duke with an expression that was both somber and confused. It was as if one moment the duke knew her and the next he hardly recognized her.

Paul quickly stepped forward while the others were distracted and reached for her hand to place a kiss upon it. "I am so glad to be home for the holidays and to have a chance to see you again, Rebecca."

She clasped Paul's hand and then covertly studied him from beneath her lashes. He stood straight and tall before her; very handsome in his dark blue double-breasted wool frock coat and tan pantaloons. He certainly appeared to have matured, but Rebecca still sensed an air of youthfulness and adventure about him which had made him such an enjoyable companion during their childish escapades.

"Lord Burton and I were discussing only yesterday how the three of us spent time searching for treasure. I told him I thought the explorations had begun when you had discovered stories of King James the first traveling through this area."

Paul laughed appreciatively as her heard her comment. "That's correct. We certainly had fun attempting to find the riches."

"Your brother could not remember if we'd ever discovered anything that was valuable."

"I believe I found a shard of old pottery and you uncovered a relatively new coin," Paul answered with a grin.

"That is exactly what I had remembered," laughed Rebecca before releasing his hand and glancing around the room. "But tell me, Paul, where is your brother? Is he not joining us?"

"The boy has no manners. He has chosen to be late," answered the duke. He withdrew from the other group to join Rebecca and Paul when he heard her query.

The duchess came bustling up behind her husband. "Frederick, remember Adrian was suddenly called away to deal with an emergency in the one of the outer fields. He returned several minutes ago. I am sure his valet Higgins is doing his utmost to quickly bring our older son to rights before he joins us for dinner."

"Yes, Father, please know that Adrian will be here as soon as he has removed the dirt of the fields from his person and is fit for company once again." Paul reached out to grasp his father's forearm before he flitted away. "Would you like me to get everyone's drinks, or would you prefer to perform the honors?"

The duke initially looked perplexed at his son's question but gradually his expression cleared. "I believe it would be best for you to perform the task, Paul. I would very likely confuse their requests."

Paul quickly determined that the ladies wished for sherry while the gentlemen requested brandy. When everyone had their drinks in their hands, he assisted his father in proposing a toast.

"Tell us all what you wish at this moment, Father," coached Paul.

"I wish all of you a very happy Christmas and a wonderful new year!"

Glasses were raised into the air and toasts were drunk. A loud knock sounded upon the door and Jennings entered the room once again. "Dinner is served, Your Grace."

The duchess turned to her son. "Paul, please take both Lady Rebecca and Miss Frost into dinner since Adrian has not yet arrived."

"Of course, Mother," Paul readily agreed and held an arm outward on each side for the ladies to grasp. "It is my understanding that Cook has outdone herself this evening. I hope you are both ready to enjoy a delicious meal."

Rebecca chuckled and lightly held Paul's arm. "I cannot consume as much food as you undoubtedly will, but I intend to do justice to Cook's culinary efforts."

"I do hope Cook has made her delicious Pigeon Compote. I confess that I am partial to that dish," admitted Miss Frost as she handed her empty glass to the maid, put her gloved hand upon Paul's other arm, and walked out of the drawing room dragging her shawls behind her.

As the group entered the large foyer which was off the entrance hall, a disturbance could be heard coming from the upper floors. "Excellent, Higgins, you have worked your magic on my cravat once again!"

"Thank you, Lord Burton. I wish you an enjoyable celebration."

"I hope it will be most memorable, Higgins. No need to wait up for me tonight. Good evening."

"Good night, my lord."

A door was slammed and footsteps could be heard hurrying across the landing.

Adrian abruptly appeared at the head of the

staircase immaculately attired in a dark green coat with a crisp white linen shirt, and a masterly tied cravat in a mathematical style, secured with a gleaming diamond pin at the front. His long, muscular legs were encased in black knee breeches. His feet were covered in soft, black leather pumps.

Adrian grinned down at his attentive audience. "Ah, I see I am just in time to lead Lady Rebecca in to dinner. I apologize to all of you for my tardiness."

Rebecca stood stock-still upon the carpeted floor her gaze focused and unwavering as she stared at Lord Burton. She would never be able to say exactly what had caused her to realize so clearly and so instantly that she was in love with Adrian. There was so much that she wanted to reflect upon and examine in this moment but her thoughts were nothing more than a disordered muddle. She forced herself to look down and study the tips of her slippers which were protruding from the edge of her gown. Then she took a few deep breaths in an effort to relax her racing heartbeat.

"I will take over from here, Paul." Rebecca heard Adrian's voice and then suddenly became conscious of his touch as he placed her gloved hand upon his arm. "You are very quiet, Rebecca. Has something occurred? Are you unwell?" he asked with genuine concern.

The sound of his deep voice so close to her ear sent shivers up and down Rebecca's spine. She was quite hesitant to speak out at that moment. Adrian read her silence as confirmation of his fears. "Paul, Miss Frost." Adrian turned to the pair immediately behind them as the others had gone on ahead into the dining room. "Rebecca is feeling unwell. I will accompany her to the terrace for some fresh air. Please inform Lord and Lady

Winton. We hope to join you shortly."

"Are you certain you wish to go outdoors?" asked Miss Frost fretfully "If you are sick, strolling outside will do you more harm than good."

"Actually, Miss Frost, I believe that is just what I need. I am afraid I drank my glass of sherry a little too fast. It has gone to my head. I am sure fresh air will put me back to rights," Rebecca assured her companion somewhat breathlessly.

"I hope you feel much improved shortly, Lady Rebecca. I will inform the others," Paul reassured her.

"I will collect your wrap from Jennings. Wait for me here." Adrian moved swiftly to the entrance hall and quickly returned carrying her pelisse. He turned to gesture to a maid who was collecting used glasses. "Millie, please accompany us to the terrace for a few moments."

"Come, this way." Adrian placed her pelisse across her shoulders and then guided her to the back of the main hall to the library. Inside the library were large, glass doors that led out to the terrace. He quickly unlatched the doors and led Rebecca outside. Millie followed them and stood back against the wall next to the house.

The cool winter air immediately revived Rebecca. She glanced up at Adrian who stood with an expression of concern, directly in front of her.

As she stared at the handsome gentleman before her, Rebecca felt her heart begin to pound once more and her palms begin to sweat. This man was her childhood friend and companion. It had been so easy to spend time with him when he was nothing more than that. Now, with her newfound knowledge of her love for

Adrian, everything had changed. How was she to speak to him as if nothing had altered? How was she to look directly at him and keep that I care for you expression out of her eyes?

"Are you feeling any better?" Adrian reached for her hands.

Rebecca twisted away from him, suddenly worried about her reaction to his touch. In doing so, the abrupt movement caused her reticule to slip from her fingers. The bag landed with a clatter upon the floor. The clasp opened and the tiny tree carving fell out.

"Oh my goodness!" Rebecca gasped and quickly reached for the carving. The item had become even more precious to her now that she had recognized the true depth of her feelings for Adrian. She stood up and examined the little tree for damage. It appeared unharmed.

"I am sorry that I startled you, Becky," said Adrian, studying her with a look of confusion. "Have I said or done something wrong?"

Rebecca turned back to him, anxious to relieve his obvious concern and bewilderment. "No, no Adrian. You've done nothing wrong. I'm sorry. I cannot say any more. I feel much better now. Will you please escort me to the dining room?"

"Not without first examining this carving." Adrian reached out and plucked the tree from her hand. He studied it intently. "Quite astonishing! I thought this was lost years ago. Where did you find it?"

"It was stuck under some torn lining inside a small chest I had made as a child," she softly replied. "Mrs. Cord had used the box to store Christmas angels in. I brought the tree tonight to ask if you remembered making it."

"And you notice that I had not forgotten." He placed the carving in Rebecca's outstretched palm. She swiftly secured it inside her reticule.

Adrian cupped her chin. He raised her head so that she was constrained to look directly into his eyes. In doing so, she forgot to shield the true and ardent emotion reflecting in them. His eyes widened in surprise as he suddenly comprehended her unspoken message. "I want you to know that I can recall anything and everything that has to do with you, Rebecca. Do you begin to understand me, my dear?"

Rebecca felt a deep glow of happiness as she heard Adrian's words. But just as quickly, she cautioned herself against jumping to conclusions. Only minutes before, she had acknowledged her love for him. Perhaps that sentiment was causing her to look for something more too swiftly from him. "I believe I do."

"Rebecca, are you ill?" Lord Winton stood at the open doors beside the maid.

She turned to face her parent. "No, Father, the fresh air has revived me. Adrian and I were just coming inside to join you," she assured him.

"Yes, everything is going to be wonderful," Adrian answered with a grin as he saw Rebecca glance up at him in some confusion as she heard his elated remark. "Let us retire to the dining room without delay."

Chapter Four

Rebecca sat on the overstuffed, mahogany-framed sofa in the summerhouse the next morning and thought about her astonishing discovery the evening before. Had the spirit of James and the admonishments the specter had raised against her been the cause of the sudden realization of her true love for Adrian? Or had she felt this way about him for a long time, confident in her belief that the deep emotion she experienced for him was something similar to the closeness one felt with a brother or a sister never realizing that it was something much more intense?

What was it the spirit had desired her to bring about? Expose the shadow that covers your deeper emotions. Allow your heart to beat freely once more.

Had the promise she'd made to the specter in the churchyard to shake the mantle of grief which still enveloped her spirit been removed so swiftly? There was definitely a new energy about her. A feeling of profound happiness made her almost lightheaded. She wanted to smile constantly or even laugh out loud.

Rebecca clasped the painting she had purchased the day before. She looked down and studied the image intently as it rested upon her lap and thought about the carefree summer days spent in the pictured meadow with Adrian and Paul by her side.

Was it too much to hope that Adrian cared deeply

for her as well? Suddenly she recalled the puzzling remark he had made to her on the first day of his return to Amersham. She had accused him of always treating her like a sister and he had answered, "Conclusions are sometimes reached without the use of common sense."

What had Adrian been attempting to tell her? Could he be implying that what she had thought was a form of sisterly affection which he had given her from the time she was a young girl had actually been a fervent and sincere regard? And what of his comments last night before they had gone in to dinner? His words made her feel that everything connected with her life was important to him.

Rebecca sighed and stood up carefully holding the painting in one gloved hand. She wrapped her paisley shawl more closely around her with the other. This time the quiet and seclusion of the summerhouse was of no help to her. Thoughts were racing back and forth in her brain with no clear answer to her dilemma coming forward. She must confront Adrian and confess her newly realized feelings to him. Nothing more could be resolved until this was accomplished.

She walked out of the summerhouse and then turned around to latch the door. The sound of footsteps crunching loose gravel on the garden pathway came to her ears. Rebecca swiftly faced forward and her heart skipped a beat. Adrian was striding through the garden coming directly toward her.

In an attempt to slow her racing pulse, Rebecca covertly studied him. His brown wool, many-caped coat was slung across his wide shoulders; his tall hat was pulled low over his eyes. The stark white of his elegant cravat stood out against the edge of his dark green waistcoat that was just visible from the collar of his coat. His hands were covered in dark brown leather riding gloves. Shiny, black Hessian boots were on his feet. He gazed intently upon the ground. His expression was thoughtful and remote.

Rebecca quickly discovered that observing the man she loved as he moved toward her was no remedy for a frantic pulse. In fact, the exercise was proving to have quite the opposite effect. By the time Adrian was a few paces away, Rebecca's heart was pounding in her ears and she was becoming short of breath. She made an attempt to speak his name.

Rebecca managed just a whisper but it was enough to capture Adrian's attention. He halted and met her avid gaze with a keen regard of his own.

"Becky!" He removed his hat before striding forward to stand before her.

"Adrian, I m-must tell you something," she began somewhat nervously. "I have recently made a very surprising discovery about myself."

"And what is that, my dear?" Adrian prompted with an engaging grin.

As Rebecca studied him, she suddenly shed her feelings of hesitancy. Adrian was her childhood companion and her dear friend. Even if he was incapable of returning her devotion, he would never chastise her for revealing her love for him.

"I love you, Adrian," she whispered, at the last moment becoming timid.

Adrian rushed forward and clasped his arms around her waist, allowing his hat to fall forgotten onto the step behind her. "I have waited so long to hear you say those words, my darling!" He bent forward and placed his warm, full lips upon her mouth. A wrenching sound came from between their compressed torsos.

"Oh, I forgot the painting!" Rebecca gasped as she regretfully moved backward, effectively halting Adrian's wondrous and dizzying kiss. "It is my Christmas gift to you."

Adrian reached down to grip the slightly damaged piece of art in his hand. He studied it intently. "Where did you find this painting? I saw one very like it at Douglas & Sons Jewelry Store. I considered purchasing the landscape because it reminded me of our adventures in the meadow."

"It is the same picture. I noticed the painting not long after you were in the shop. Young Mr. Douglas said you had also expressed an interest in it. I purchased the painting for you as a Christmas gift for that same reason—happy childhood memories."

Adrian turned and carefully placed the picture on the step next to his discarded hat. He then moved to face Rebecca once again. He reached inside his coat and brought out a gaily wrapped, oblong box. "This is my gift for you, Becky," he said softly as he placed the item in her hand.

Rebecca smiled shyly up at her companion. "It appears that I was not the only one who found an appropriate gift for the festive season"

"This is something I have had for a long time, my dear. I decided it was the right time to present it to you," he answered her somewhat mysteriously.

Rebecca bent over the package once more and eagerly removed the wrapping. She pulled the lid off the box and gently moved the paper away from the contents. "Oh, my goodness, it is my long-lost treasure! How did you find it, Adrian?"

"You put it inside my shoe for safe keeping one day during one of our picnics. We both forgot about it, I wore the shoes home and never found the coin when I went back to look for it. I discovered it on the floor of my closet a few months later. I decided to keep it and surprise you with it sometime in the future." He reached inside the box and gingerly lifted a necklace out. A slightly tarnished shilling was encircled with silver and a tiny clasp on the edge then attached to a delicate chain. Adrian placed the empty box upon the step and then moved to face Rebecca once more.

"Turn around, my dear; I will put the necklace on for you. I waited a little longer than I had originally intended, but now we both have items that will bring us happy memories of our childhood."

Rebecca enjoyed the feeling of Adrian's warm hands at her nape before twisting around to allow him to admire the trinket. "Thank you so much for my gift."

Adrian reached forward to clasp both of her hands in his. "You have made me incredibly happy, Rebecca. I will treasure the picture that you gave me, my dear." He moved forward to place another warm kiss upon her lips.

Too quickly, Adrian raised his head, sighed, and dropped her hands. He then got down upon his knee, heedless of her protests. "We must return to the main house momentarily, my dear. I have spoken to your father for permission to pay my addresses to you. Both your parents were delighted with my request and Lord Winton graciously gave his consent. However, Lady Winton only gave me ten minutes alone with you before she threatened to send Miss Frost to join us. So I assure you of my total and complete love and devotion for you. And I wish to formally request that you, Rebecca, my one and only love, become my wife."

"Yes, of course, I will marry you, Adrian. I love you so very much." Rebecca placed her hands upon his shoulders. "Now please stand up. I want another kiss."

****

Christmas Eve morning

Rebecca left her horse in Jacob's care and walked to the churchyard gate. Once inside she moved to stand at the foot of James' grave. She studied the inscription intently again before reaching for the locket. She placed it at her feet. The token began to glow as soon as it came in contact with the ground.

"Rebecca, you have returned." The unearthly sound of James' voice reached her ears as she felt the now familiar blast of cold air against the side of her face. "I was hoping to speak with you today."

"I promised that I would return Christmas Eve morning, James," she replied suddenly hesitant to relate her joyous tidings to the spirit.

"Have you broken free of the sorrow which has surrounded you since my death?" the specter sighed into her ear.

"James, I have discovered that I love Adrian," she admitted breathlessly.

Silence greeted her pronouncement. Several moments passed before the sound of the spirit's hushed voice became apparent once again. "I'm very pleased to hear this. Have you told Adrian?"

Rebecca raised her head to gaze at the gray clouds above her. "Yes, I have told him. He said he loved me too and proposed to me. I-I have agreed, James."

"I'm delighted. Not only have you freed yourself from the intense sorrow which choked all life and vitality from you since my death, you have also come to acknowledge your love for Adrian which, but for my presence in your life, you would have recognized a long time ago."

Rebecca lowered her head and stared at the ground once again. She'd heard James' words but she was confused by them. "I don't understand what you're telling me. You believe that I loved Adrian when I was promised to you?"

"You loved him, but you didn't recognize the emotion for what it was. You felt you cared for him like a sister. Soon after I asked your father for permission to pay my addresses to you, I sensed the closeness between you and Adrian. I realized that we could never experience that kind of intense emotion together.

"I loved you with a superficial emotion. You are beautiful, intelligent, and we had common interests. I cared for you but the love Adrian had for you went far deeper and was much more lasting than any emotion I was capable of feeling for you."

"At first, when Adrian approached me and insisted that I give him my word that I would always care for you, I assured him that he had no cause to worry. I even became angry when he continued to push me for my pledge."

Rebecca started in surprise when she heard this comment. "I remember coming upon the two of you when you were arguing."

"Yes, I recall that day. He mentioned something about my trying to control his life for him when we sensed your presence and you appeared satisfied with his explanation and placed no importance on our disagreements at that early stage of our friendship. Soon after, Adrian and I came to an understanding about our various attempts to advise or control the other man's life. We agreed to allow each other to live our lives as we saw fit. We became very close friends.

"Meanwhile, I used the fact that I had joined my regiment and was expected to join the fighting against Napoleon in France any day as a way to postpone our nuptials."

Rebecca gasped in surprise when she heard this comment. "I thought we were waiting to become man and wife because you were concerned you might die in battle and leave me behind with few memories of our married life together to comfort me."

"That was what I intended you to believe. In reality, I knew that I could never give you the deep-seated love and devotion that Adrian had for you, and I was postponing the inevitable, I suppose, telling you that we could never be married."

"I'm sorry that you felt that way, James. I never experienced any qualms about marrying you while we were betrothed."

"Which in a way, shows that something good has come out of my death. You have discovered your intense affection for Adrian. He obtains the woman for his wife who he has loved deeply since childhood."

The spirit suddenly made a noise that sounded like a grunt. "Are you still with me, James?" she asked with concern.

"I must leave you quite soon. Before I go I must thank you. Your happiness is my salvation. I can now rest in peace. But I want you to know, in my own way, I did love you, Rebecca."

"Goodbye. Goodbye, James," she called out as the locket shone brightly for a moment more before returning to its normal state.

"Rebecca, my dear, who are you talking to?" Adrian walked to her side and gently grasped her arm.

Rebecca turned to her betrothed and studied Adrian's concerned expression. She had no doubt that he loved and trusted her. Would he believe her tale? She quickly decided to take the chance.

"Adrian, I have spoken with James' spirit here at his graveside for the past few days. His specter was restless and unable to find peace. He said this was because I had broken my promise to him that I would not waste my life lamenting his loss. Also, my friends and family were concerned about my continued mournful manner."

"You actually heard James' voice?"

"Yes, I did. At first, I was afraid. I stood here and pleaded with the spirit to convince me that what was happening was real and important."

"The apparition was able to convince you to believe?"

"Yes. The specter soon persuaded me of its existence and advised me to break free of the shadow which covered my deeper emotions since James' death. It counseled me to allow my heart to beat freely once more."

"You hadn't been yourself for a long time."

"I realized how much I had held myself back since James' death. How controlled my emotions and my day-to-day life had become. It was when I made a promise to change the melancholy and downcast person I had become to someone who enjoyed life again, that I came to recognize my love for you, Adrian."

He wrapped his arms around Rebecca. "What did you discuss with the specter today, my love?"

"James knew something that I never realized. He cared for me but understood that the love you had for me went far deeper than any emotion he was capable of feeling. He also said that something good had come from his death—my recognition of my love for you and your ability to win the woman who you have loved deeply since childhood."

Adrian bent down to kiss her lips. "James' spirit has given us the greatest Christmas gift of all, the gift of love."

Better Than
a Present

by

Cynthia Moore

Holiday Series

Dedication

"Being deeply loved by someone gives you strength,
while loving someone deeply gives you courage."
~Lao Tzu

Chapter One

London, late spring 1818

It was the third occasion she had noticed him at a ball that Season. Miraculously, this time he stood in the queue to request an introduction from her aunt and possibly inquire if he could partner her in one of the upcoming sets. Regrettably, her dance card was full. The last space had been filled in moments before by a short, portly gentleman named Mr. Sidney Bass who was a particular friend of her Aunt Grace.

Managing to keep a cheerful expression on her face, Lady Samantha Grayson placed her hand on Lord Torrington's sleeve, the gentleman who was to be her partner in the next quadrille, and turned away from the crowd of eager suitors with a sigh of frustration. Out of the corner of her eye, she saw the man who had so piqued her interest turn away and walk toward the doorway.

As Samantha moved to her place before the quadrille began, she was conscious of an ache in her chest that made it hard to breathe. She realized there was moisture forming at the corner of her eyes. She looked down at the floor, blinked the tears away and attempted to dispel her intense feelings of disappointment by deliberating on the cause of her attraction to the unknown gentleman. He was undeniably attractive; tall, athletically built, with thick black, slightly wavy hair, high cheekbones, and a firm chin gracing a lean, chiseled profile. From the start, she had been fascinated by the deep blue color of his eyes when she'd discovered him studying her intently from the edge of the dance floor at Lord and Lady Redwood's ball a few weeks before. Samantha had been eager to discover the man's identity from that moment. She had intended to inquire if her aunt was acquainted with the gentleman and beg an introduction but her plan was quickly foiled by that lady's announcement that she would take Samantha and her sister Sara to another party that evening. They had left the ball minutes later.

Samantha placed her gloved hand on top of Lord Torrington's and then curtseyed to his bow as the dance began. Her thoughts were far away from her activities. For some unknown reason she felt a special connection to the elusive gentleman. The second occasion she had noticed him had begun with nothing more than a casual glance across the room. She spotted him strolling in a group of people moving toward the main door of the establishment. Moments later, he had left the party. They had exchanged fleeting looks at each other before he abruptly departed. Even with such momentary contact, Samantha knew instinctively this was a man she would like to become acquainted with.

Without knowing him or actually speaking to him, she could somehow sense he wasn't concerned about following society's strictures or rules. Not that he was outwardly snubbing people or conducting himself without style or manners. To the contrary, on the three occasions that Samantha had seen him, he appeared to be relaxed and unhurried, polite to all who spoke to him.

He lacked the nervous, panicked demeanor of so many of the gentlemen she had been introduced to this Season.

This commonplace attitude was very trying as well as frustrating when attempting to carry on an intelligent conversation. Additionally, Samantha found herself unable to fully concentrate on the discussion when confronted with a gentleman who kept twisting his head around to avoid poking himself in the eye with his heavily starched shirt points. It was also quite disappointing to discover one's dance partner had nothing of interest to discuss with her other than the possibility of rain on the morrow.

Something told her that this man was different. She had noticed his skin was lightly tanned by the sun so she imagined he enjoyed spending most of his time outdoors. He also wore his clothes with a casual grace. He radiated a classic, elegant type of sophistication. There was no need for him to be encumbered by impossibly high shirt points or brilliant, flamboyant colors on his waistcoat that were currently favored by many who were intent on outdoing each other with the hope that their audacity would bring the notice of the Season's prized young ladies in the famed *marriage mart*.

Rather, he chose to avoid drawing comment by wearing clothing with a subtle dignity and, in the short period of time Samantha had demurely scrutinized him, she noticed that this habit as well as his friendly, amiable manner caused his acquaintances to treat him with obvious respect and admiration.

Samantha had long ago acknowledged that she greatly valued her own independence. She loved spending as much time as possible outdoors. On days when bad weather kept her inside, she loved to read books describing the native trees and flowers of Great Britain. She had a secret wish to someday visit Cornwall and see the lovely gardens there by the sea. Granted, a young, unmarried woman had to conform to many of society's strict guidelines. Until this spring when she had finally agreed to have her Season with her younger sister, Samantha had managed to indulge herself in these enjoyable pursuits and avoid the *beau monde* milieu with the constant round of visits, events, outings and balls that one was required to attend when one resided in the city of London.

****

Lord Paul Russell bowed to his hostess and thanked Lady Forester as he accepted his hat from the butler who hovered nearby. Placing the hat upon his head, Paul nodded to the servant, walked out of the opened door and strode down the marble steps to the street.

He sighed with great disappointment as he moved away from the Forester mansion. There would be no more opportunities this Season to be introduced to the lady who had attracted him from the moment he saw her dancing a waltz at Lord and Lady Redwood's ball a few weeks earlier. This afternoon he had received a summons from his steward at his small estate of Windmere in Saltash, Cornwall to return as soon as possible because a recent downpour had caused major damage to some outbuildings and walls near the inlet. His steward needed him to see the actual destruction and to determine how he wished to proceed with the repairs.

Paul had had high hopes that he would at least have been able to secure a dance with Lady Samantha Grayson tonight. He had managed to learn her name when he overheard a spiteful, seemingly jealous lady bemoaning her popularity with the other eligible gentlemen as he stood waiting patiently to sign her dance card this evening.

Now it was his turn to lament the lady's well-favored attraction. He had arrived at the ball almost unfashionably early tonight only to be waylaid by Lord and Lady Everard who were very close acquaintances of his parents'. It would have been extremely boorish as well as bad-mannered to have brushed off their inquiries about his family in his haste to discover Lady Samantha's whereabouts.

By the time he finished his conversation and made his way to the ballroom, he had found his quarry surrounded by a crowd of eager gentlemen waiting to request a dance with the lady. Not one to cause undue attention to himself, Paul joined the group and serenely stood by for his opportunity to speak with her.

A few moments later, his disappointment was acute as Lady Samantha indicated her dance card was full. She turned away from the remaining multitude of crestfallen gentlemen to join the quadrille with her extremely fortunate dance partner at her side.

As he began to come to terms with his keen feelings of frustration over missing his chance to become acquainted, he deliberated over the reasons for his powerful attraction to Lady Samantha. To be certain, she was a beautiful woman. Her heart-shaped face, full red lips, sparkling emerald eyes, all framed by abundant auburn hair swept up into a generous cluster on the crown of her head had drawn him to her in the beginning.

Until he had spotted her waltzing at the Redwood's

ball, Paul had been unhappy with the current crop of eligible women he had met during the Season. He was tired of the simpering, coy young misses who seemed to dominate the group. Whenever he had attempted to carry on an intelligent conversation about something other than the weather with these women, Paul was met with blank, uncomprehending looks or simply breathy, nervous giggles often followed by timid, witless agreement to his question or statement.

For some reason, Paul had a sense that Lady Samantha would be different. In the few occasions he had observed her, Paul never saw her acting like a shrinking violet. She held herself with a confidence that told him she was quite comfortable with the way she was and not unduly concerned or nervous about finding a gentleman to marry her.

He also had the impression that she had a refreshing interest in the world around her and he was certain if he had had the opportunity to chat with Lady Samantha, their conversation would have been lively as well as interesting. He had observed her conversing with several people and he had noted that she appeared to carry on her discussions with acumen, using direct eye contact and giving all of her attention to the person or persons she was speaking with.

Paul could also discern that Lady Samantha was an outdoor person. Not only did he notice her skin was lightly bronzed by the sun, he also sensed a healthy vitality about her that was lacking in so many of the other women he had met. Spending time outside was important. Not only did he enjoy taking long walks and rides, he often assisted his head gardener in planting new trees and flowers on his estate in Cornwall. He was weary of the languid, droopy qualities he found in ladies who spent most of their time indoors.

Paul took a deep breath and exhaled with a sigh as sensations of intense regret at his failure to secure an introduction to Lady Samantha this Season engulfed him. As he climbed the stairs leading to his lodgings to collect his belongings in preparation to leaving London, he wondered if there was any chance the lady would remain unattached and available the following Season.

****

Christmas Eve

Samantha regretted her choice of borrowed garments. The snow storm appeared suddenly without warning on Christmas Eve morning. To make matters worse, the horse acquired from her brother-in-law's stables had taken exception to the frigid, icy weather and bolted, leaving Samantha dazed in an untidy heap on the newly-fallen frozen slush with a backside that was becoming more uncomfortably cold and wet by the minute.

Samantha struggled to stand and sighed as she watched the mare disappear over the rise of the hill in front of her. She was stuck out in the middle of the deserted woodland without any prospect of an immediate return to the snug confines of her sister's home. The animal was certainly headed back to the protected warmth of the stables. She grimaced as another bit of cold snow found its way inside the collar of the bulky groom's coat she was wearing. She stamped her feet in loose boots and slapped her hands encased in overly-large gloves against her legs that were covered in a roomy pair of breeches in an ineffective attempt to keep warm. She peered anxiously out from under the brim of her floppy hat for any sign of shelter.

****

The original idea for her adventure hadn't seemed so fraught with concerns and hazards. Samantha simply wished to get away on her own for a while; outside in the fresh air for a quick morning ride, before it was time to dress in her finery and the afternoon's Christmas Eve festivities began. She wanted to escape from her deliriously happy, newly married younger sister, Sara, Lady Dixon. Sara met her husband Lawrence Appleton, Viscount Dixon at a ball in London in early May. Never mind that it was Sara's first Season. The pair had quickly fallen in love and married just two months later.

Now Sara wanted nothing more than the same kind of happiness for her older sister. Sara was concerned over Samantha's continued unwedded state at the advanced age of twenty-four. From the moment Samantha arrived at the Dixon country estate in Berkhamsted accompanied by her maid several days before, Sara had done nothing but discuss and consider various options for a plan that would allow Samantha to meet the man of her dreams and assure her own joyful union before too many months had passed.

At first, Samantha tolerated Sara's well-meaning attempts to find her a potential husband. But as the days went by and Sara hadn't stopped talking about the subject or listened to Samantha's opinions on whether she believed she could ever find a man to love as Sara had, Samantha began to feel trapped. In the beginning, she listened to her sister with tolerable amusement but now Samantha was becoming angry and frustrated. It wasn't as if she hadn't had her own Season albeit at an advanced age. Samantha was twenty-three and Sara had turned nineteen when they both had their Seasons together.

When Samantha was eighteen years old and Sara was barely fourteen, their parents, the Earl and Countess of Grayson had been killed in a carriage accident. Their family had been extremely close and the sudden loss of their beloved father and mother had been terribly hard for Samantha and Sara to accept. The girls moved in with their aunt, Lady Grace Anson in London when their own home had passed to the heir, a distant cousin from Scotland.

After the year of mourning for their parents passed, Samantha turned down her aunt's offer to chaperone her during the Season when she was nineteen. She still felt deeply saddened by her shocking loss and not ready to put on a glowing smile for the stipulated number of balls and parties she would be required to attend. Instead, Samantha informed her aunt that she would prefer to wait until Sara was of age and take their Seasons at the same time.

Just a few months previously, Samantha and Sara had each been presented in Court and gone to a number of events in London. Samantha had met many amusing gentlemen and handsome lords but none had spawned any lasting interest and certainly no one had stolen her heart in the way that Sara appeared to feel about her new husband. Her thoughts drifted back to the mysterious gentleman who had commanded her attention a few months ago. She often found herself mulling over the reasons for her continued preoccupation with him. She had to admit to herself, he was the only man ever to bring forth such intense sensations of regret and disappointment inside of her when she considered her failure to secure an introduction to him. She consoled herself with the thought that if the two of them were meant to meet, the occasion would surely have occurred before her Season ended.

When June arrived, Samantha had had more than enough of the never-ending amusements and she decided to set up her own house. She was perfectly happy at present living with her old nurse Mrs. Simms and her maid, Bertha in a small cottage her father had left to her on the outskirts of London. Surely she was old enough to decide how she wanted to live her own life? Her sister needn't act like she knew Samantha better than she knew herself!

In this crabbed and discouraged state of mind, Samantha had decided to escape the confines of her sister's home and go for a morning ride. The evening before, she convinced Bertha to procure a pair of boy's breeches, a shirt, coat, boots, gloves and hat from the grooms' quarters inside her brother-in-law's stables. Bertha reluctantly complied with her mistress's request and early this morning, just as the sun was rising, she helped Samantha struggle into the groom's outfit.

She was gratified to discover that the items of clothing Bertha collected fit her small frame tolerably well. All except the boots fit loosely but without any need for adjustment. Samantha stuffed a stocking inside the toe of each of the shoes and judged them quite comfortable for her purposes. She instructed her maid to meet her at the rear kitchen door in three hours' time with a change of clothes; judging that her safe return would lessen the severe scolding her sister would no doubt give her if she discovered what Samantha had done before she got back to the house.

The sky outside her bedchamber window was clear with the faint outline of many stars. Samantha instructed Bertha to fasten her long auburn tresses securely to the crown of her head. Satisfied that her hair was anchored firmly in place, Samantha clamped the cocked hat down so it hung low over her forehead just above her eyes. With a silent nod of thanks to her apprehensive maid, she picked up the boots and tiptoed out of the room in stocking-covered feet.

When she reached the entry at the bottom of the main stairs, Samantha paused momentarily to look for any sign of Grimm, the butler. She breathed a sigh of relief when she detected no sign of activity. She had counted on the fact that the servants would be preoccupied with many extra tasks required to prepare for the Christmas Eve celebrations that afternoon.

Samantha moved stealthily down the hallway and quickly opened the door to Viscount Dixon's study. The curtains were closed and the room was still dark. She took a deep breath in an attempt to slow her racing heartbeat. If her brother-in-law had chosen to come down early for some reason, to be discovered dressed as she was would mean certain disapproval and an end to her plan of temporary escape. Pausing only to put her feet inside the pilfered boots, she walked on tiptoe to the French doors leading out to the rear garden. Moving as soundlessly as possible, she pulled back the curtains, released the latch and stepped outside. After carefully closing the doors behind her, she covertly made her way down the path that led to the stables.

Upon arriving at the building, she nervously opened one of the side doors. She heard the raised voices of several men in an adjacent room arguing about the care and feeding practices for one of the Viscount's prized horses. She took advantage of the grooms' distraction and moved quickly to a nearby stall where she knew Mable, a trusty reliable old mare resided.

Mable was languidly chewing on a clump of hay when Samantha entered her domain. The mare turned an indulgent eye on her and stood still as she placed a saddle on Mabel's back and then tossed the bridle over her neck; adjusting the iron bit in the mare's mouth.

Samantha led Mable outside to a nearby tree stump. Using this as a platform to stand on in order to gain the necessary height to allow her to put her leg over the horse's back, she arranged herself in the saddle, secured the reins in her hands and then nudged the mare's flanks. Mabel ambled away down the path and the sound of the men's discussion gradually faded away.

After a few minutes, Samantha became accustomed to the singular sensation of riding a horse astride. She liked the feeling of control when one's legs were hugging both sides of the animal. She took a deep breath of the cool, crisp morning air and was prepared to enjoy herself on this brief respite away from her meddling, busy-body sister.

She'd gone only a short way when a strong, icy-cold wind rustled the bare branches of the nearby trees. Ahead dark gray clouds marred the sky that had been clear a short time before. Minutes later, fluffy white globs of ice began to obliterate her view of the trail ahead and several snowflakes fluttered down to land upon Samantha's nose.

She studied the frozen slush as it fell against the branches of the stand of trees in front of her. She deliberated whether she should continue on. She reminded herself that the sky had been clear not long ago. The storm would surely pass in short order. She wouldn't end her ride so soon after all the trouble she had gone to in order to accomplish it. Samantha urged Mabel on with a stern but soothing tone of voice. She was hopeful the snow wouldn't last and create only a light dusting of powder on the bleak landscape. The mare responded to her commands at first but as the weather worsened, Mable became more and more intractable until she finally wedged her front hooves into the now snow-covered ground and refused to budge. A moment later, she found herself tossed into the cold, wet slush and she watched as Mabel cantered away from her, back to the warm comfort of the horse stables.

As she peered through the now rapidly falling snow flakes, Samantha sighed with relief. Just ahead of her appeared to be a small cottage. She could vaguely make out dark, painted planks of wood and the outline of a tiny window framed with curtains on the side of the rustic building. The most promising feature was a steady stream of white, puffy smoke escaping from a rotund chimney at the front of the cottage. Someone was inside with a fire burning in the hearth. She could imagine how wonderful the warmth from the flames would feel on her chilled skin.

She took a hasty step forward and then paused. The chances were very good that one of the occupants inside the dwelling would be a man. No lady would inhabit such a lonely place on her own. At present, she was a woman dressed in a man's outfit. Other than the clothing, she had taken no real pains to make herself look like a true gentleman. If the person inside the building was alone, would she be able to make him believe she was a groom who got lost in the woods? Her teeth began to chatter as a swirling cloud of icy snow whistled past her face and the decision was made for her. She lifted her sodden boots and made her way through the slush to the front porch of the cottage.

A loose floor board on the stairs creaked under her shoes and the front door of the building was thrust open.

"Adrian," a cultured voice rang out, "I asked you to leave me alone for a few hours!"

Samantha stopped moving and stood on the porch as the owner of the voice stuck his head around the open door.

"I promise to return…uh, sorry, you're not Adrian."

Samantha gulped and stiffened in shock as she stared at the tall, handsome young man with thick, tousled black hair, firm chin, high cheekbones and long, aristocratic nose who stood peering out at her as she paused with one foot balanced on the edge of the step. It was the same gentleman who had piqued her interest in London! She was too far away to see the color of the man's eyes but she knew from the previous memorable encounter with him on the crowded ballroom floor that they were a deep blue. Those same beautiful, haunting eyes now focused on Samantha with a kind of intensity that made her feel cautious and uncertain about her reception. The gentleman was not dressed in the formal attire that she was used to seeing him wear in London. Tight-fitting pantaloons hugged his muscular thighs. His feet were covered in muddied, black boots. He wasn't wearing a coat; his shirt was unbuttoned at the throat and his cravat was untied, hanging loosely across the front of his broad chest. In one hand, he held what appeared to be an open flask.

"Come in, come in. Don't dawdle…lad. Warm your frozen bones by the fire."

Samantha hesitated. Was it possible he remembered seeing her in London? Could he have recognized her through her disguise? She convinced herself that the attraction she felt for the gentleman was certainly one-sided. Granted, he had initially joined the crowd wishing to sign her dance card at the Forester ball. But when he had failed to secure a dance, he had left without attempting any further contact with her. Surely he wouldn't have cause to question the fact that she was not a groom even in her hurriedly-donned costume? Another cold, wet snowflake lodged itself inside her coat's collar and she shivered. Logs burned in the hearth and she thought of the comfort the fire would bring to her frozen limbs. There was no possible way she could walk away from his invitation.

Chapter Two

Paul took a hasty sip of brandy.

The lady who had so recently occupied many of his dreams stood in front of him dressed provocatively in men's pants, a coarse white shirt, floppy hat and rumpled jacket. There was no doubt in his mind. It was Lady Samantha Grayson; the woman he had fantasized about from the first evening he had spotted her across the crowded dance floor in London.

He had a gut feeling that if he let her know he knew who she was, dressed in such a manner, it would embarrass her. There was also a real chance she would turn and run away from him to avoid any further humiliation. He couldn't have her dashing outside with a good prospect of becoming lost in the woods in this weather. He stood back and opened the cottage door wider.

He forced himself to keep his face devoid of all expression as she moved toward him. In her haste, and no doubt hampered by the large boots she wore on her feet, she pitched forward, landing with a thud against his chest.

He reached out and put his free arm across her back to steady her. He could feel his heart begin to race at the close contact. "Careful...boy, we can't have you coming to harm as well as catching your death in this snow storm. Sit down by the fire and tell me what you're doing out in this frigid weather."

He led her forward into the sparsely decorated room. A dilapidated old sofa faced the fireplace. His discarded coat lay on top of one of the cushions. Three wooden chairs were lined up against the back of the sofa. A small table with the remnants of a mince pie and a loaf of bread, and a small cupboard were the only other pieces of furniture occupying the space.

"Take off the coat and your other wet things. Put them on this chair. I'll draw it up to the fire. We'll have them dry in no time. Your boots can probably stand a little warmth as well." He put the flask on the table and held out his hand as he waited for her to do his bidding. It would be interesting to see how she handled the situation.

She started to remove her hat and then suddenly lowered her arms.

"Come on, lad, you're not getting any warmer standing there in those wet clothes."

"I...uh, my ears are cold. I want to leave my hat on," she answered in a forced, gruff voice.

He stood without moving for a moment after she had spoken. He was debating how compelling he should be with her. Hopefully she wouldn't catch a chill by leaving the sodden garment on her head. But then again, she probably knew if he saw her long hair, he would realize she was a woman. He cleared his throat as an image of long, auburn tresses flowing down across Lady Samantha's back came to mind. "Uh...suit yourself, boy. Hand me your coat and gloves then."

Gingerly, she pulled the loose-fitting, wet garment from her shoulders and handed it to him. Then she turned away to yank the gloves off. She dropped them to the floor and stuffed her bare hands into the side pockets of her pants. "My boots are fine."

Paul looked away from her to hide his sudden grin. He had glimpsed her small, feminine hands just before she tucked them in her pants. He imagined she had stuffed something inside the boots to make them fit better. That explained her refusal to hand them over to him.

He draped the coat over the back of one of the chairs and moved it closer to the fire. Then he picked the gloves up off the floor and tossed them onto the hearth. He placed the other two chairs at the table. He imagined she was hungry. "Sit down, lad and help yourself to what's left of my mince pie. There's a piece of bread too."

She walked toward him, nodding her head in an effort to keep the floppy hat down low on her forehead almost covering her eyes. "No, thank you, sir, I'm not hungry."

"Have a sip of brandy then. It will warm your insides." He thrust his open flask under her nose.

She didn't answer and made no move to touch the container. He assumed she was trying to keep her replies to a minimum as well as continuing to hide her hands from his sight.

"Look, I need to go outside for a moment and check on my horse. He's in a small, covered shed out back. Help yourself to whatever you want." He capped the flask and dropped it onto the table. Then he went to retrieve his coat. There was no way she would eat or drink anything as long as he hovered nearby.

"Sh...should I come out and help?"

"No, no, I simply want to make certain he is

comfortable. It wasn't snowing when I arrived. You stay here. Eat something and get those clothes dry."

The back door squeaked on its hinges as he yanked it open and stepped outside. Cold, wet snowflakes obliterated his view. He made his way to the shed and found his large, black stallion Cornelius munching on a pile of hay.

The horse stopped eating and raised his head to study him with what he imagined was a look bordering on indignation. Cornelius would take him to the ends of the earth with no complaint, but being housed in this rickety outbuilding in the middle of a snowstorm was substantially beneath his horse's dignity. He spotted an old blanket hanging on a peg in the corner of the room, spread it open and tossed it over Cornelius' back.

"There, that should keep you warm. The storm shouldn't last too long."

The horse snorted and turned his attention back to his food. Paul chuckled and patted the horse's thick mane before turning back to the cottage.

"Whoa, boy, be careful how much you swallow of that brandy," he called out from the doorway as he heard Lady Samantha begin to cough. She put the stopper back in and dropped the flask onto the table. She stood and turned her back on him as she continued to choke.

"A couple good wallops should set you to rights." He couldn't resist striding across the room and thumping her on her back.

"Th...thank you, sir, I'm fine now," she replied hoarsely. Her coughing subsided. She wiped her eyes and stuffed her hands back into the pants' pockets before turning around to face him once again.

"It appears you haven't been around liquor too often

in your life. How old are you, boy?" He was curious to see how she would answer his question.

"Tw…twenty-four," she mumbled.

"You're small for your age. I would have guessed you were younger." He answered her straightforwardly as something told him she had given him her true age. "Look, it's still snowing outside. We're going to be here for a while. We might as well keep each other company. Have a seat. What's your name, lad?"

"Sama…Sam," she muttered as she sat on the battered sofa.

Paul moved one of the chairs close to her, sat down and faced the fire, inwardly amused by Lady Samantha's quick-thinking adjustment to her name. "My name is Paul. This is the game keeper's cottage on my brother's property Burton Keep. The man has gone away for a few days to visit his sister for the holidays."

She remembered something he had mentioned earlier. "Is your brother's name Adrian?"

His eyebrows raised in surprise. "How did you know that, Sam?"

His name was Paul. She could clearly see his deep blue eyes that were framed by thick black lashes. That meant he had a clear view of her face as well. She lowered her head under the floppy hat and spoke in as deep a voice as possible. "You said something about Adrian leaving you alone for a few hours when I arrived."

"Oh, yes, I had forgotten. When I heard footsteps outside I assumed it was my brother coming to pester me."

"Why would Adrian want to annoy you?"

He sighed before he spoke.

"My brother is Adrian Russell, Marquess of Burton. Adrian recently married Lady Rebecca Hastings of Amersham. Rebecca was a childhood friend of both myself and my brother. Her father is the Earl of Winton. Our father is the Duke of Haverston. We grew up on neighboring estates."

The heat from the fire began to warm the skin on her chilled face. She was conscious of the smell of the leather on the boots as the sodden surface began to dry. She scrunched her wedged toes inside of the shoes and was gratified to discover they felt almost normal once more. Even though the brandy had made her cough, it certainly helped to lessen her sense of apprehension. She was relaxed and less concerned about the precariousness of her position. "Your brother and Lady Rebecca are married, Lord Paul?" she asked, peeping out at him from under her hat while still remembering to disguise her voice.

Paul frowned down at her. "Let's do away with the title, lad. There is no need to be formal in this situation we find ourselves in." He paused and ran a hand through his hair and pursed his full lips before answering her question. "Yes, they are. That's why I'm here hiding from Adrian and Rebecca. They were married three years ago right after Christmas and are now expecting their first child. They are both giddy with happiness and want the same bliss for me. Adrian has informed me they intend to host a party soon after the New Year and invite all the eligible ladies and their families from neighboring estates. Adrian and Rebecca are very hopeful I will meet my true love at the event."

Her heart beat rapidly as his words resonated in her mind. *He was in the same situation she herself was in;*

well-meaning family members were attempting to force him into marriage so that he could hopefully experience the same state of euphoria they themselves had found. Didn't they understand it wasn't that easy to stumble upon someone you could fall in love with? That it wasn't something to be pressured into?

"W...was their betrothal something planned in their youth?" She asked gruffly.

"No, not at all; Adrian and I both looked upon Rebecca with sisterly affection for most of our youth." The flames from the roaring fire reflected with a golden glow on Paul's forehead and created shadows on the sculpted, curved angles of his cheeks. "I believe Adrian fell in love with Rebecca after he spent some time with other young ladies in London. He informed me that no woman could compare to Rebecca before he left for Cambridge that summer." He paused as a gust of wind rattled the front door. "I should check on the weather."

He stood up and walked to the front window. He pulled back the curtain and studied the outdoors intently for a few moments. "There are only a few flakes falling at present. We should be able to return soon if the storm is truly over. By the way, Sam, I never asked where you came from. Were you walking? I assume you're in Viscount Dixon's employ?"

She didn't answer him at first while she went over her options in her mind. It was imperative that he not discover her true identity. Should she tell him she worked on another estate? The problem was, she wasn't familiar with the area and didn't know other family names. And she must rely on him to see her back to her sister's home. Without a horse of her own, she had no choice. "Y...yes, I am. I...I was exercising a horse when the storm began. The mare took exception to the weather and dumped me in the snow."

"Will you be missed? Will someone be sent to search for you?"

She couldn't help but shiver as a vision of her brother-in-law riding up to the cottage inquiring after her came to mind. How awkward that situation would be! She crossed her fingers inside her pants' pockets as she answered, "No, no, they will assume I found shelter."

"What about the horse?"

"The mare is old and very set in her ways. I'm sure she has returned to the stables."

"Very well," he placed another log on the fire and then moved toward the table.

She covertly studied him as he picked up the flask. He took a swig of the brandy before turning around and offering the container to her. She lowered her head as she mumbled a refusal.

"We were discussing Adrian and Rebecca's joyful union. As I mentioned, their own happiness gives them license to wish the same for me. So here I am hiding away from their good intentions. What about you, lad? Do you have any well-meaning family members who are attempting to force you to settle down?"

She wished she had taken another sip of the brandy. How to reply to his questions? She was supposed to be a groom employed by Viscount Dixon. Naturally, most grooms had families; certainly many had brothers and sisters. Should she make up a plausible tale that mirrored her own personal experiences and frustrations? Perhaps sticking as close as possible to the true story would make matters less confusing.

"Uh...well, my parents were killed in a coaching accident several years ago. I do have a sister who has recently married," she admitted.

"Is she pressuring you to find a woman to marry as well?"

"Um...I'm a little young to consider starting a family. I need to work hard and save my money before I can think of getting married. But you are correct. My sister is frequently touting her happiness to me," she answered breathlessly as she struggled to complete her longest reply as yet to him while still keeping her voice disguised.

"So you can relate to the situation I'm going through with Adrian and Rebecca. I know that I should agree to meet these ladies from the neighboring estates. And I have to concede with Rebecca when she says I will never find my true love if I don't make an attempt to meet eligible, unmarried women. But I have been to London during the Season and I have mingled with the available damsels in the *marriage mart*. I found many pleasing daughters of peers and some lovely young widows as well. But I haven't met anyone who sparks a lasting interest in me let alone a woman I could see myself falling in love with."

She held herself in check as she listened to his laments about his efforts to find a lady to love. He didn't mention being attracted to any particular woman in London. He hadn't taken any special notice of her during the Season or felt the allure that she held for him. She couldn't help feeling a sense of despair at the thought. Interestingly, in every other aspect, his experiences practically mirrored her own except his parents were still alive. She wondered if they were concerned about his unmarried state as well. "You haven't mentioned your mother and father. Are they prompting you to find a lady to marry as well?"

"No, my father's memory is no longer sharp. He does know who I am but any concern about my current bachelor state wouldn't be something that would register in his mind as an issue to worry about. Naturally, my mother is extremely happy about Adrian and Rebecca's marriage. And especially now that Rebecca is increasing, she sees no reason to rush me into a hasty union that I might regret in the future." He hesitated a moment before speaking again. "Do you believe in love at first sight, Sam?"

Out of the corner of her eye, she could see that he had turned in his chair and was looking directly at her. She kept her face forward and her hat low over her forehead as she focused her gaze straight ahead at the stone fireplace. For some reason, she felt it was important that he understand her answer to his surprising question. "No, not at all; how could anyone make such a silly declaration? I suppose I could believe in attraction at first sight. I can understand experiencing a special connection with someone you have just been introduced to but how could it be possible to love a person that you don't know?"

"Rebecca claims she loved Adrian from the time she was a child without realizing she felt such an intense emotion for him. It took really looking at him when he came into a room unexpectedly to come to the sudden, startling revelation that she was deeply in love."

She forgot to keep her face averted and turned to stare at him when he spoke those words. Her heart was pounding and she felt flushed. She had a sudden sensation that something important was taking place in that moment. In a quest for an answer to the cause of her feelings of confusion, her eyes focused on his deep blue ones before she realized that she was allowing him a clear view of her face. As she became aware of what she had done, she looked away and forced herself to act relaxed as if nothing momentous had just occurred. She uttered the first question that came to mind. "W…what about you? Do you live in the area as well?"

He raised his eyebrows and sat up a little straighter in his chair when he heard her question. "No, I don't. I have a small estate in Saltash, Cornwall called Windmere."

"Cornwall!" Samantha blurted out the word in surprise.

"Yes, have you been there?" He looked confused by her reaction.

"Uh…no, I've never visited Cornwall but I have often wished to." She still made the effort to disguise her voice but answered in a much softer tone than before.

"Cornwall can be quite beautiful in the spring when the flowers are blooming and the trees are full and green with their new leaves," he spoke with pride.

"Believe me, I know how lovely the area can be," She adjusted her tone to a gruff whisper once again.

"I thought you said you had never been there," he pointed out in a puzzled tone of voice.

"I…I love to be outside with the horses but I…I also love plants."

"Do you have a small garden at your home?"

She started to reply and then stopped herself. A groom would never be able to afford a house. She thought for a moment before speaking, "No, no, I live in a tiny room off the stables. The head gardener is my friend. He allows me to potter around in my employer's garden when I have free time."

"How did you learn about Cornwall?"

She studied Paul's handsome profile from under the brim of her hat before she answered his question. She couldn't help but admire his firm chin and full, kissable lips. She turned away and refocused her thoughts as she felt her heart begin to pound faster in reaction to his attractiveness. "Ah…the gardener has a few books on the gardens in Cornwall. I have studied them."

"So you can read. Where did you go to school, boy?"

"My…my mother taught me. She was schooled by our parish priest." She felt herself getting in too deep as the falsehoods she was telling began to mount. She attempted to turn the conversation back to him. "Tell me about the gardens at Windmere."

"I have a formal rose garden, a tree-lined walk that runs alongside an inlet, a small maze and large grassy area in front of the house."

She closed her eyes and imagined his garden as he described it to her. She could envision the colorful rose bushes blooming in the spring and the green, leafy trees bordering the path. How lovely it must be! "You are very, very lucky to own such a place."

"You know, there is a chambermaid who works at my brother's home who I think would be just the woman for you, Sam. I've noticed she spends most of her free time strolling in the gardens at Burton Keep. Come on over after the holidays and I'll introduce you."

Chapter Three

Paul detected the note of reverence in Lady Samantha's voice when she complimented him on his home even though she was still making a great effort to disguise it. It was clear she placed a high value on the simple beauty of flowers and plants. A deep sense of contentment settled over him as he realized the two of them had much in common.

He hadn't been able to resist tormenting her with his last comment about the chambermaid. He was eager to see how she would handle the situation.

She made no reply to his barb and rose from her seat. "I…I'm going to check outside."

He studied her as she strode across the squeaky floor in the over-sized boots and reached for the handle. After opening the door, she thrust her hand back into her pocket and walked out onto the front porch. He could see her taking deep breaths of the icy cold air.

He stood up. "How does it look out there?" he called.

"The…the sky is clear. There is very little snow on the ground. I think it has warmed up."

He joined her on the porch. "Good; must have been a freak snow storm." He put his hand on her sleeve. "Look, I'm sorry that I mentioned the chambermaid, Sam. I should have realized that you want to be left alone to make your own decisions on who you want for a loving companion and wife just as I do. I won't say any more about it."

She continued to face the frozen landscape. "Thank you."

"We should be able to make our way back now." He moved away from her. "Come inside and get your coat and gloves. I'll tidy the place up and then take you back to Viscount Dixon's stables."

She put on her over-sized coat and placed the bulky gloves on over her hands while he was busy cleaning up the remnants of the pie and bread. Then he banked the remaining glowing embers in the fireplace making certain it would not restart itself after their departure.

He took one last look around the room and then locked and secured the front door. "Let's go."

Paul led her outside to the back of the cottage where a small shed was standing. He pushed back the thin door on the building to reveal a large, black stallion that took up most of the inside space. "This is Cornelius. He might look fierce but he is actually a lamb at heart. You ride up behind me. He can easily carry us both."

"Uh...if you're sure."

He moved an empty crate that was propped against the wall closer to Cornelius. He looped the bridle over the horse's head and adjusted the bit in his mouth. "Let me climb on first."

He put one foot in the stirrup and swung his other leg over the stallion's broad back. He adjusted himself until he was sitting to the front of the saddle tight against the pommel. He gently pulled on the reins as Cornelius started to prance. He leaned forward to whisper some calming words to the horse and guided him next to the crate once again.

"He doesn't understand the shift of weight. He'll get used to the awkward sensation in a moment. Go ahead, step here and get your leg over, lad."

She stood up on the crate, wobbling slightly as her feet shifted inside of the loose boots.

He reached out with one hand to steady her. "Careful."

She hoisted herself up and onto the stallion's back.

He led Cornelius outside of the shed. He could sense that she was gripping the sides of the saddle. She shifted her weight and landed against him.

"Hold still, Sam. We're in tight quarters here," he instructed her through gritted teeth. "Grab my arms. I don't want you falling off."

After a few seconds of hesitation, she gripped both of his forearms.

Cornelius trotted through the melting snow and made short work of the distance she had covered with Mable a few hours before. Beyond asking once if she was comfortable, Paul was quiet throughout the ride. Her nearness was distracting him and he wanted to make certain they arrived at their destination without further mishap.

A few minutes later, the horse trotted up the rise of a hill and the Dixon stables were visible below them.

"Please let me off here. There is a stump over there that I can use to dismount."

He guided the horse over to the protruding piece of trunk. He held Cornelius in check until she carefully lowered herself off of the horse's back. He waited until her boots touched the solid ground to speak.

"Merry Christmas, Sam! I enjoyed talking to you."

"Same to you, sir. And thank you."

With nonchalance he was not actually feeling, he casually waved his acknowledgement of the words of gratitude and turned his horse around the other direction toward Adrian's estate. As Cornelius plowed swiftly through the rapidly melting snow, he found himself taking several deep breaths to attempt to calm his shaking hands and his wildly beating heart.

Sam, ha! It had to be her! Those bulky clothes did nothing to hide feminine curves and she walked with a woman's inherent grace. Her speech was too cultured for a groom as well even though she had made a valiant effort to disguise the sound of her voice. And those dark green eyes; they were the same that had mesmerized him when Lady Samantha Grayson had happened to gaze directly upon him at Lady Redwood's ball.

Now, unbelievably, he had spent much of the morning alone in her company. He went over their conversation in his mind. He was charmed as well as intrigued. Granted, he imagined she was holding herself back from saying too much in hopes that he wouldn't discover any flaws in her disguised voice. But even so, their discussion left him excited, inspired. They had so many things in common. He was very eager to spend more time with her.

He also had a premonition that her skittishness today had not only been from concern that he would discover she was a woman dressed in groom's clothes. He was fairly certain she was reacting to his presence. He knew she had noticed him in London. Paul gripped the reins tightly at the thought of Lady Samantha being attracted to him in the same way that he was captivated by her. He found her equally enticing dressed in baggy men's clothing as he did when she was beautifully clothed in satin ball gowns.

He sat up straighter in his saddle as he spied another man on horseback coming toward him. If he wasn't mistaken the gentleman was Viscount Dixon himself. He was just the person Paul wanted to see.

****

Samantha kept her head down and walked as quickly as she could to the door leading to the kitchen at the back of the house. The morning's events were beginning to take a toll on her. The stress of acting the male part without any preparation in front of Lord Paul had been exhausting. Despite the pleasurable time she had in his company and the intense attraction she was beginning to feel for him, she was eager to return to the comfort of her brother-in-law's home and resume her true identity.

She reached for the latch, pulled it open and stepped inside a small room containing muddied boots and various cloaks hanging on hooks protruding from the wall. Her maid entered the room just as Samantha yanked off her coat.

"My lady, there you are!" Bertha looked worn out and she gushed in a nervous manner as she clutched Samantha's change of clothing in her hands. "I was worried when the storm came up! And then I heard tell that a horse had returned to the stables with the saddle but no rider!"

"My horse took exception to the weather and tossed me. Thankfully, no harm was done. I found shelter," Samantha answered her maid, relieved to speak with her own voice once again. "Where should I change? Does my sister know I've gone?"

"In here, my lady." Bertha indicated another door

nearby and opened it. "It's the housekeeper's sitting room. She's too busy this morning with the holiday preparations to be concerned about us using it. And no, Lady Dixon believes that you're still in bed."

She slipped inside the room. Bertha followed shutting the door firmly behind her. "Sara accepted an excuse like that? She knows I never linger in my bed in the morning unless I'm ill."

"I took the liberty, my lady, to inform Lady Dixon that you had some trouble falling asleep last night and would join her later in the morning."

"You did well, Bertha. Sara wouldn't question that logic." Samantha sat on the edge of an overstuffed chair and raised one booted foot toward her maid. "Pull these things off me. My toes are beginning to hurt."

In short order, her maid removed the boots and the rest of the borrowed clothing.

Samantha donned fresh undergarments and then her maid lifted a mint green muslin morning gown over her head. The sash was tied at the back and matching kid slippers were placed on her tired and sore feet.

Her maid studied the front of the garment with a frown on her face. "Your gown has a wrinkle at the front where I grabbed it in my haste to find you, my lady. Should I press it for you?"

"No, no, there is no time. I will be changing in a matter of hours for the Christmas Eve celebrations so this dress will suit me fine until then."

"Yes, Lady Samantha. Please sit on the chair again, my lady. I need to brush out your hair and refasten the pins."

Several minutes later, Samantha was ready to face the others. She opened the door to the housekeeper's quarters and peered outside. No one was visible. She turned back to her maid. "Return the groom's clothing as quickly as you can. I'll be in the breakfast room."

"Yes, my lady."

Samantha walked toward the kitchen nursing her bruised toes. She sniffed the air appreciatively. Now that she was free of her disguise, she was able to relax and savor the delicious smells of the traditional Christmas dishes. The heady fragrances of roast beef, goose and gingerbread all combined to make her almost empty stomach rumble with hunger.

She strolled around the corner into the room and surprised the cook, Miss Mott as she was cutting up some squash.

"Oh, my lady, I wasn't expecting you! Is there something I can get for you?" the cook asked as her face flushed with a rosy hue.

"No, no, I was simply enjoying the delicious aromas coming from the kitchen."

"Why thank you, Lady Samantha. I trust the food will taste as good as it smells."

"I'm certain it will."

With a parting smile to Miss Mott, Samantha made her way to the breakfast room where she found her sister finishing a piece of toast.

"There you are. Are you recovered from your lack of sleep?"

"Yes, thank you, Sara."

"You'll have to help yourself to the eggs, ham and toast this morning. Grimm and the other servants are busy supervising the placement of the holly and laurel sprigs in the drawing room. I have requested a kissing bough to be hung in the center of the room as well. I thought it would be amusing."

Samantha filled her plate with eggs and ham and sat down at the table. She poured herself some tea adding milk and sugar. "You're just looking for any excuse to kiss Lawrence, Sara."

Sara blushed before retorting, "Don't forget, Aunt Grace and her newest conquest Sir Chester will be arriving very soon. I'm certain they will take advantage of the tradition as well."

"Oh, yes, our aunt will definitely pluck a few berries from the kissing bough. She was never one to turn down an embrace from her admirers." Samantha smiled as she thought of Aunt Grace's many gentlemen friends. She was a lovely, vivacious woman in her fifties. Her husband had been killed in a hunting accident over ten years ago. She had had a steady string of suitors since coming out of mourning but she never seemed to wish to settle down with one man in particular.

"It's too bad you don't have a special someone who can join you this evening," Sara sighed.

Samantha grunted indelicately as she heard her sister once again lament the fact that there was no important man in her life. She started to reply and thought of Paul. She looked up from her plate to stare out of a nearby window. The time she had spent with him and the discussions they had that morning now seemed imaginary, as if it was something she had dreamed. She refocused her gaze on her sister and quickly answered, "We have been over this before. I'm perfectly happy as I am."

"So you say. You don't know what you're missing," her sister rose from the table and pushed back her chair.

"I'm sure you're sick of hearing me go on and on about the subject. It's Christmas Eve so I'll refrain from saying anymore for a few days."

"Thank you." Samantha sighed with relief. "I know you only have my best interests at heart."

"I believe it would be more proper to say your happiness is my concern. Enough of that for now. I'll leave you to finish your meal in peace. I'm off to make sure all the preparations are going smoothly. I'll see you later, Samantha."

Samantha pushed away her plate of unfinished food after Sara left the room. She wasn't hungry anymore. Her thoughts focused on Lord Paul. She realized, with a deep sense of regret, there was no chance she could further her acquaintance with him. He believed she was a groom in Viscount Dixon's employ. What reason could he ever have to wish to continue a discussion he had had with a minor servant while waiting out a snow storm? Additionally, if he were to see her dressed as a lady in the near future, there was a good chance he would recognize her and her deception would be discovered.

Her heart felt heavy in her chest as it became apparent to her that she had finally met a man who she enjoyed talking to, a gentleman who made her pulse beat faster whenever she looked at him or came in contact with him. But she could not make herself known to him. To do so would ruin her reputation. What occurred today would have to become nothing more than a pleasurable memory.

The door was thrust open and an attractive woman with abundant brown hair slightly streaked with gray tucked under a jaunty red cap, burst into the room. "My dear Samantha, there you are. I have missed you so!"

"Aunt Grace!" Samantha was enveloped in a heavily-perfumed hug and then released. "I'm very glad to see you as well."

"Meet Sir Chester Booth, Samantha. Chester, dear, this is my other niece, Lady Samantha Grayson."

A tall, dignified gentleman with a thick crop of gray hair on his head and a gentle smile on his face paused on the threshold and bowed. "A pleasure to meet you, Lady Samantha."

She curtseyed to the gentleman. "I'm very happy to make your acquaintance, Sir Chester."

"We met your sister in the hallway. She is quite busy overseeing the preparations for this afternoon," Lady Anson remarked as she took off her fur-lined pelisse and dropped it on a nearby chair. "I imagine it is quite important to her to have the Christmas Eve celebrations go off without a hitch. It is her first major event as hostess since her marriage."

"Yes, I'm sure Sara wishes to prove that she deserves to carry the title of Viscountess Dixon while at the same time hoping to make her new husband proud of her. Are your rooms prepared? Would you like to sit down and have a cup of tea? There are some ham and eggs left. I could request Cook to heat them up for you."

"It would be lovely to have some refreshment. Chester, dear, put your coat over here next to mine. Grimm is seeing to our bags. We'll go up to our rooms after we have a spot of tea. Maybe Chester would like a bit of ham?"

"I'll take a slice. No need to heat it up, though."

Samantha poured the hot liquid into two cups. "How was the journey?"

"Uneventful until it suddenly started to snow. We were worried we might be forced to spend the night at an inn, were we not, Chester?"

Sir Chester frowned as he heard the question. "I was somewhat concerned over the state of the roads but the storm seemed to pass as quickly as it started and our coachman had no problems."

"The countryside is quite beautiful here. Have you had a chance to take any walks around the area since you arrived, Samantha?" Her aunt stirred in milk and sugar and sipped her tea.

"Yes, I have. I agree with you, Aunt. Even in winter, the woods surrounding the house are very lovely."

"I seem to recall...Burton Keep is close by, isn't it?"

"Yes, it is the nearest property to the north. Are you familiar with it?"

"I have never visited there but I have a loose connection to the owner. I believe Adrian Russell, Marquess of Burton resides there. Your late Uncle Robert was close friends with his father the Duke of Haverston."

Sir Chester spoke up. "My dear, you're correct. I had forgotten Burton Keep was located in Berkhamsted."

"I think I heard that Lord Burton was married a few years ago. I can't remember the lady's name."

"I believe you are thinking of Lady Rebecca Hastings."

"Yes, that's right, Samantha." Her aunt beamed at her. "I wasn't aware you were acquainted with her."

Samantha realized she had made a comment

without thinking of the ramifications. "Oh, I have never met the lady or Lord Burton. I...I did some research on the estates in the area and found their story quite interesting."

"I believe the viscount and his wife were childhood sweethearts?" Her aunt was not about to let the subject drop.

"They grew up together, yes. But I'm not certain when the attachment was actually formed," Samantha prevaricated.

Sir Chester drank the rest of his tea and cleared his throat before speaking. "I think I recall that Lady Rebecca was previously engaged to the Earl of Archly. He was killed in the Battle of Waterloo."

Lady Anson reached across the table to affectionately pat him on the cheek. "Wonderful, my dear. I remember the story now. A trifle sad but overall quite lovely and romantic in the end, I believe. But Lord Burton had a brother, let me think...Paul; Lord Paul Russell is his name. I had heard that he was in town during the last Season. Unfortunately our paths never crossed. I remember him as a pleasing, handsome young man. I was looking forward to introducing him to you, Samantha."

Thankfully, Samantha wasn't required to reply to her aunt's startling comment. At that moment, Sara entered the breakfast room.

"I'm sorry that I did not greet you properly when you arrived, Aunt Grace, Sir Chester." Sara gave her aunt a hug. "Grimm has seen to your bags. You are both welcome to rest in your rooms before we gather for the festivities in a few hours."

"I believe I will retire for a short time before I dress

for the evening. Long journeys do wear me out."

Sir Chester came to his feet and assisted their aunt as she rose from her chair. "Some delicious smells are coming from your kitchen, Lady Dixon. I look forward to this afternoon's meal."

Sara smiled warmly. "Thank you so much for your kind words. My cook, Miss Mott and I have tirelessly worked on a special menu for the holiday. I hope you will enjoy it."

"If the aromas are anything to go by, I'm sure I will."

Lady Anson put her hand on her swain's sleeve as they prepared to leave the room. "We will see both of you later then."

"Yes, Aunt, I will have Grimm take care of your coats."

Samantha and Sara observed the couple as they strolled out of the room. Just before disappearing around the doorway, they saw their aunt smile up at her companion and bat her eyelashes at him in a coy manner.

"It looks as if Aunt Grace plans to do more than rest in her room before dinner," Sara commented with a grin.

For some reason, Samantha had an image of Paul as he threw his arm wide to catch her when she tripped over the threshold at the cottage. She relived those moments when she was cradled securely against his muscular chest.

"Lucky, lucky lady," Samantha replied with a sigh before she too walked away from her astonished sister and exited the room.

Chapter Four

The dining room glistened in the warm light cast by two large silver candelabras placed at either end of the long table. Gleaming white porcelain dinner plates framed by well-polished silverware lay in front of each of the guest's chairs. Empty crystal wine goblets sparkled invitingly at each plate. The table itself was covered in a white damask tablecloth. Sprigs of holly, rosemary and laurel were artfully scattered across the middle of the surface.

Samantha slipped into her place at the table. She was tardy getting to dinner because just as she was leaving her bedchamber, Bertha had asked her advice on whether it was proper for her to respond to some advances a footman from the Dixon household was making to her. Samantha had offered her maid her opinion on the predicament but it had caused her to be late arriving at the dining room.

She took a moment to study the festive decorations with appreciation. Sara should be proud of herself and her staff.

"Is anything the matter?" her brother-in-law asked from his seat at the head of the table.

"No, no, my maid needed some advice on a personal matter. I'm sorry to be late." Samantha frowned in consternation as she realized that her tardiness caused him to worry.

"To the contrary, I believe you are just in time," Lawrence's thick blond hair shone brightly in the candle light and a diamond pin sparkled from his intricately tied cravat as he grinned at Samantha.

The door to the dining room opened with a flourish and Grimm entered carrying a large platter containing sliced roast beef surrounded by potatoes and squash. Two other servants followed in his wake; one carried a carved, cooked goose with stuffing and the other bore a large silver vessel from which a sweet and spicy smelling steam arose.

"Ah," Sir Chester sniffed the air appreciatively. "The Wassail Bowl, I believe."

Grimm carefully supervised the placement of the dishes. The Wassail Bowl was set on a nearby side table. The butler put the roast beef down in front of Lord Dixon. The goose was placed near Sara. Then Grimm picked up a heavily-decorated silver ladle and lowered it into the bowl of spiced wine and roasted apples. The other servants brought over the empty glasses. The butler carefully and deliberately spooned the warm wine into the crystal goblets while the guests helped themselves to the feast on the table.

When everyone had been served both food and drink, the viscount rose from his chair. He picked up his wine glass and saluted Sara.

"To my wife, Lady Sara Dixon, who has worked resolutely over this past week with our cook, Miss Mott and our butler, Grimm to ensure we begin the holidays with this extraordinary Christmas Eve meal. Thank you, my dear."

Sara raised her glass as well. "You're quite welcome, Lawrence. It was a delight planning my first holiday meal in my own home. I hope you all enjoy it."

Samantha, Aunt Grace and Sir Chester all stood up and raised their glasses in unison. Samantha spoke first. "Happy Christmas to everyone; you did extremely well, Sara."

"Everything looks delicious. I'm very proud of you." Lady Anson smiled at Sara.

"It's been a long time since I saw such a spread," added Sir Chester, enthusiastically. "Thank you so much for including me in your invitation to visit your home for the holidays, Lady Dixon."

Everyone settled back in their seats and applied themselves to the meal. The tone of the conversation was lively and happy. Sara pointed out the new ruby necklace that her husband had given her and Lord Dixon brought notice to his new diamond stick pin that Sara had presented to him just before dinner.

"Sir Chester was kind enough to give me this bauble," Aunt Grace preened as she turned her head so they could all get a view of the sparkling jeweled comb that was securely anchored at the crown of her head.

"My hands will never be cold again. Lady Anson has provided me with a pair of handsome fur-lined gloves," Sir Chester announced with an appreciative grin directed to the lady at his side.

"I wish to thank Sara and Lawrence for the beautiful beaded reticule you both gave me." Samanthasmiled warmly at her sister and brother-in-law.

"You're welcome, I thought the reticule would go well with most of the colors you seem to favor," Sara acknowledged her sister's words of thanks. "You look very beautiful in the gown you are wearing tonight as well."

Samantha looked down at her new deep green satin gown that exactly matched the color of her eyes. The sleeves were full and tapered; the neckline fashionably low. She had wanted a new dress for the holidays and had been lucky enough to find a bolt of this luscious green material in London. She had splurged and spent some extra pin money on the fabric and had a dressmaker who was currently all the rage in the city make the gown for her. She completed her festive outfit with a pearl necklace that had been her mother's and dainty pearl earrings that Sara had given her on her twentieth birthday dangled from her earlobes.

"I agree; your dress is lovely. You must tell me the shop in London where you found such a pleasing shade of green satin." Her aunt beamed at her from her seat across the table.

"It's at a mercer's called Ford, on Piccadilly, Aunt."

"I know of that shop. I will make a point to visit there soon."

"I want to thank you for the extremely soft satin nightgown you gave me as well."

"I hope you enjoy it, my dear. I find wearing smooth, silky garments such as the one I found for you can actually relax me and provide me with a better night's sleep," Aunt Grace commented with a sly grin at Samantha.

"I must say that all the ladies look beautiful this evening." Lawrence took a sip of wine and cleared his throat. "If everyone has finished their meal, I would like to make a suggestion. Because this is Christmas Eve, I propose that Sir Chester and I forgo our after dinner brandy and we join the women in the drawing room for a game of Blindman's Buff."

Aunt Grace clapped her hands and laughed merrily. "I haven't played that since I was a young girl."

"Is that the one that requires a blindfold?" Sir Chester frowned in confusion.

"Yes, that's right. We determine one person who is 'it'," Lawrence replied. "They are blindfolded and the rest of us move around the room occasionally poking or buffing the person who can't see. They must attempt to grab one of us as we pass by. When someone is caught, 'it' must guess who has been captured. When a correct surmise is given, the trapped individual becomes the new 'it'."

"Are you certain we have enough people to make the game a challenge?" asked Samantha somewhat skeptically.

"I remember playing it as a youth with my three other cousins. You quickly learn how important your sense of touch is when you can't see. Even so, I recall that it was quite confusing to determine which cousin was actually near me because as soon as I thought I knew, someone else would move in. And remember, the person must be caught before you can make a guess."

Sara giggled and stood up from her place at the end of the table. "I should enjoy playing the game, my dear. I'll instruct Grimm to bring the gingerbread and butter shortbread to the drawing room along with the brandy and tea."

"Gingerbread as well?" Sir Chester questioned with great enthusiasm. "You have excelled yourself, Lady Dixon."

Samantha got up from her seat and placed her hand on Sir Chester's sleeve as he came to a stop by her chair with her aunt hanging onto his other arm. The three of them followed Lawrence and Sara down the hallway to the drawing room.

A large fire fueled by a huge log burned merrily in the massive fireplace. Garlands of holly and laurel hung on the mantel and framed the walls of the room. In the center, a kissing bough gaily decorated with many white berries and sprigs of mistletoe hung from the chandelier.

"Ah, wonderful, but we must make certain the height is correct," Lawrence led his wife to the middle of the room and promptly gave her a kiss on the lips underneath the bough. He reached up and pulled one white berry down and placed it in Sara's hand. "Exactly right, my dear."

"I'm glad, Lawrence." Sara gave her husband a tender smile.

Sir Chester hastily dropped Samantha's arm leaving her standing just inside the room. He guided her aunt forward. "I'm never one to miss such an opportunity."

Sir Chester took his time with his kiss and Lady Anson certainly wasn't complaining. She appeared to savor his embrace and give herself up to the enjoyment of it until he slowly backed away. "My goodness, that was quite something, Chester," her aunt exclaimed somewhat breathlessly. She looked dreamily up at her swain as he dropped a white berry into her hand.

Samantha studied the two happy couples from her vantage point in the doorway. Once again her thoughts strayed to Lord Paul and the time they had shared together that morning. She missed his warm smile and his pleasing company. It would be wonderful to have him here and to be able to kiss him under the bough.

"Here is Grimm with the blindfold. Why don't you go first, Samantha?"

Samantha flinched as she heard her brother-in-law's voice. She had been lost in her own daydream and hadn't been listening at all.

"You want me to start?" she frowned at the piece of black cloth Grimm held in his hands.

"Yes, don't be shy, Samantha," Lawrence teased her. "I'll wager you capture one of us before too much time has passed."

"Remember this is the first time I have played this game. Be kind to me." She giggled and held still while Grimm tied the blindfold over her eyes.

She found she agreed with Lawrence's earlier statement as Grimm guided her forward. Without her sight, her sense of hearing was certainly heightened. She was very aware of the slightest noise; clicking of heels on the wooden floor, the cracking and popping sounds of wood burning in the fireplace, and the swishing sound of her dress as the material caressed her legs when she shifted around the room.

Grimm stopped moving and Samantha stood still, waiting for some sound from the others or a perception of movement around her.

Moments later something bumped her arm, she felt a caress on her shoulder, and then a gentle nudge on her elbow. She reached out and touched nothing but air. She turned and brushed against some soft material. A woman's muffled giggle reverberated in her over-receptive ears. *Aunt Grace!* Samantha thrust one arm out to the side in a sudden, quick movement. Her fingers made contact! She held on tightly and squeezed what felt like thick, woolen fabric.

"I've got you!" She realized she was gripping a man's arm and was aware of rigid, firmness as she held onto what was apparently the sleeve of a gentleman's coat.

Obviously, she had captured either Sir Chester or Lawrence. It was hard to believe her brother-in-law would allow himself to be caught so early in the game. "I know you are a man," Samantha announced confidently.

She slowly moved her fingers up the sleeve. She gripped the heavy material. Samantha had an immediate sensation of power and strength as her hand came in contact with a muscular forearm. *It had to be her brother-in-law.*

"It's you, Lawrence," she declared proudly. "I'm surprised you made it so easy for me."

"No, no, it's not me."

She froze with her hands in mid-air. She had been about to remove the blindfold. "Sir Chester?"

"Incorrect again."

She lowered her arms to her side. "I'm very confused. Did you bring Grimm into the game without telling me?"

"No, he has left the room."

Samantha stood still as she heard Lawrence's reply. Then Sara giggled and Sir Chester cleared his throat. Heavy footsteps resounded on the floor and then stopped.

"I believe it is time we removed the blindfold," her brother-in-law's voice pierced the sudden silence.

She looked down toward the floor as gentle fingers worked the knot free at the back of her head.

"See who you caught," Sara's excited voice rang out in Samantha's ears.

She took note of gleaming black leather shoes

topped by dark gray trousers hugging a pair of muscular legs. Without a doubt, this was a gentleman. She quickly raised her head.

"Paul?" She clamped her hand over her mouth as she realized she had spoken out loud. It was him! He was here in this room; the man who she had admired from afar in London, the man who occupied her thoughts almost exclusively over the past few hours and the most daunting fact of all, the man she had kept company with that morning dressed as a groom.

"Hello, Sam…Samantha."

His deep voice resonated throughout the room. He had purposely said Sam before calling her by her own name. He knew who she was. He had seen through her disguise. Samantha slowly lowered her hand from her mouth. She stared into his shining blue eyes. She studied his full, smiling lips. Her heart began to beat erratically and she felt light-headed. She suddenly recognized the sensations she was experiencing for what they were. She was in love.

Without further thought, she reached out and pulled Paul toward her. She placed her hands on his shoulders, looked purposely up at the kissing bough dangling above their heads and then placed her lips on his.

He had no qualms about kissing her back, she thought with pleasure moments later when he dropped a white berry into her palm. She stared up at him with a dreamy expression on her face.

"Um, I believe the two of you have some things to discuss. You may use my study for a few minutes."

Lawrence's voice recalled her to her surroundings. She looked around the room and saw Sara grinning happily from her seat close to the hearth. Her husband stood behind her with his hand resting on Sara's shoulder. He was also smiling at Samantha. Sir Chester and Aunt Grace sat close together on the sofa holding hands. Her aunt was beaming across the room at her and Sir Chester appeared to be casually winking one of his eyes. Certainly none of them acted surprised at Paul's sudden appearance. She remembered her earlier conversation with Bertha that had caused her to be late arriving at the dining room. Something told her that discussion had been planned just for that purpose.

"Shall we, Samantha?" he held out his arm and she placed a somewhat unsteady hand on his sleeve.

He led her out of the room and down the hallway. Samantha silently pointed to the closed door that led to the study. He opened it and guided her into the chamber.

Leaving the door slightly ajar, he turned to her. He was quiet and simply stared at her for several seconds. "You look very beautiful, my dear. I imagine you have several questions you wish to ask me. Should we sit down?"

Feeling quite unsettled as well as tongue-tied, she merely nodded her head and walked across the room to sit in one of the high-backed chairs that faced the windows. She started in surprise as he bent down on one knee before her.

"Wh...what are you doing?" she gasped.

"Before we get too far in our discussion, I have something important to say to you." He studied her face intently. "I wish to ask you to be my wife, Samantha."

"I...I" she stopped. She couldn't speak. Paul's statement had taken her breath away.

"I want you to know," he continued in a deliberate, serious tone of voice, "that I am asking this of you not because you have been compromised when you spent time alone with me and your family expects me to come up to scratch but rather, as unbelievable as it may sound, I have fallen totally and completely in love with you and wish to spend the rest of my life with you by my side as my partner and wife." He reached out and stroked her arm.

"I...I feel as if I'm dreaming." She found her voice and stared up at him in wonderment.

He smiled down at her. "This is reality, my dear. I noticed you in London last spring and I felt attracted to you even before I saw your beautiful green eyes and observed your confident, enthusiastic manner. Unfortunately, we never had the chance to be formally introduced and I left the city extremely disappointed, wondering what could have been if we had met and if you would still be available next Season. This morning, when I looked out of the cottage door and saw you dressed in groom's clothing, I couldn't believe my luck. I resolved not to waste the chance I had been handed to spend time with you and to talk to you."

"Oh, my goodness, Paul, I had no idea." Samantha finally found her voice. She felt tears pricking her eyelids as she pointed to a nearby chair. "Please, get up off the floor. Come sit down."

He settled himself next to her and clasped her hand in his own. "What do you say to my proposal, Samantha?"

She hastily wiped the moisture from her eyes with her free hand and turned in her chair to face him. "I, too, was captivated by you in London. I also wished to meet you. Today when I saw you at the cottage, I was nervous and excited at the same time. I was nervous because I knew it was imperative that you not guess I was a woman. My excited feelings came because I felt I was being handed a chance to discover if you were the man I had been searching for as a perfect complement to myself.

"When I returned here and thought more about you and our discussions, I missed your presence and wanted to be with you again. That is when I realized I couldn't see you because I thought you believed I was truly a groom. To show myself to you dressed as a lady would risk harming my reputation. I felt I had lost the opportunity to know you better."

He chuckled. "You obviously hadn't practiced walking like a man and no matter how bulky the groom's clothing was, it could never hide your womanly shape from my eyes."

"So you knew from the beginning?"

"Oh, yes. But I realized if I admitted I saw through your disguise you would immediately take flight and head back into the storm. I couldn't risk you getting lost in the snow and I wasn't about to pass up the chance to be with you."

"I assume you were in my brother-in-law's confidence?"

"Yes, I was. Shortly after I dropped you at the stables, I encountered Viscount Dixon. He had been told by his staff that a saddled mare had returned to the stables without a rider. He originally conjectured someone had tried to steal the horse and for some reason, the mare had bucked them off. Lord Dixon had ridden out to comb the nearby woods looking for an injured person. I told him what had actually happened, guessing at the reason you disguised yourself and left the house on your own."

She giggled. "You realized the tale I told about my sister being recently married and pressuring me to start my own family wasn't far from the truth?"

"Even in the short amount of time we had together, it quickly became apparent to me that you wouldn't be comfortable with anyone attempting to control any part of your life."

She studied his handsome face with a look of surprise on her own. "You do know much about me, don't you?"

"We have a special connection. I have been aware of it since I saw you standing on the porch in those floppy boots this morning." He raised her hand to his lips and kissed the soft skin on her palm.

Samantha felt her cheeks flush and her heart began to race at his touch. "Wh…what about this evening? Did you plan the surprise?"

He grinned. "I knew I couldn't show up and request an introduction. You wouldn't have agreed to see me because you thought I would realize I had seen you earlier this morning dressed as a groom. I had to appear without you knowing I was there. Lord Dixon came up with the idea to play Blindman's Buff."

"I was never more astonished in my life when I looked up and saw you standing in front of me."

He gently clasped her fingers in his hand. "The kiss you gave me told me that you were very glad to see me. But you haven't answered my question, Samantha. Will you marry me?"

"Oh, yes, yes, yes! I would be much honored and quite ecstatic to be your wife, Paul! It's funny; we had discussed love at first sight. I knew without question that

I loved you when I raised my head and saw you standing before me tonight."

"Ah, Samantha, you have made me the happiest of men." He bent down and gave her a lingering, very satisfying kiss.

"Now, now you two lovebirds, it's time to join the rest of us and have some gingerbread."

Samantha reluctantly moved out of Paul's arms and turned toward the sound of her sister's voice. "Oh, hello, Sara. Please meet my betrothed Lord Paul Russell."

Sara grinned as he stood and bowed to her. "That is wonderful news, Lord Paul. I was worried that my sister would never find a man to make her happy."

"I intend to keep her as content and blissful as possible during all of our married life," he vowed.

"Now I clearly understand why you were so insistent that I find a man to love, Sara," she stood up and smiled at him. They held hands and followed her sister as she walked out of the study. "There is truly no better feeling in the world."

Paul stopped moving as they reached the hallway and turned to look down at Samantha. "This happened so fast. I'm sorry that I have no ring or Christmas gift for you."

Samantha studied Paul with a tender smile upon her face. "The gift of you for a lifetime is infinitely better than a present, my dear."

It's Never Enough

by

Cynthia Moore

Dedication

To my daughter, Emily.
The advice you give is invaluable and priceless to me.
I love you.

Chapter One

December 23, 1815

"Ellie! Miss Worth! Please wake up!" Lady Selina Durwood gripped her maid's shoulder.

"What...what? Whatever is the matter, my lady?" Ellie sat up in bed and pushed her cap back off of her forehead.

Selina placed her hands over her belly and moaned. "I'm famished. I can't sleep. My stomach is growling like an angry bear with a bee in its ear! You need to accompany me to the kitchen."

Ellie yawned loudly and then looked embarrassed. "I'm sorry, my lady. We were traveling all day to get here and I ate a huge meal in the servants' quarters this evening. I'm plumb exhausted as well as stuffed. Are you sure you're hungry?"

Selina walked back into her own room and reached for her wrapper. She tied it securely at her waist and thrust her feet into the slippers near the bed. "You know what has happened lately whenever I go to balls or parties and I have to sit at a table and eat food surrounded by people I don't know. I get nervous. I worry someone will ask me a question just as I take a mouthful of meat. Or a piece of cabbage will get stuck in my teeth and it will shine like a green beacon for everyone to see when I smile. I end up taking a few small bites before the hostess rises from her seat and announces it is time for the women to leave the gentlemen to their brandy and cigars. Such a thing occurred tonight."

Miss Worth sat up in her cot and frowned at Selina from the connecting room. "But, my lady, Lord and Lady Dunstable have been friends of your parents since before you were born. And you've known Lord Rockton for many years. Surely you have no trouble eating a meal around them?"

Selina began pacing across the carpet that lay in front of the hearth. She needed some sort of activity to keep her mind off her hunger pains while she waited for Ellie to get ready. "Of course I don't. But several new acquaintances are joining us here for the holidays. A Lord John Bartley, his sisters, Miss Bartley and Miss Frances Bartley and Lord Bartley's friend, Sir William Elsmere. They were all at the table this evening."

Miss Worth struggled to her feet and thrust her arms into her wrapper. "Oh yes. I believe I heard the butler mentioning the arrival of more guests. He seemed very upset that Lord Crestor hadn't made an appearance, my lady."

"Robert...um, Lord Crestor? He is busy with the Cavalry Brigade in Brussels. He can't make time to be with us now." Selina stopped pacing and frowned down at the glowing bits of coal in the hearth.

"But, my lady, Napoleon is safely imprisoned on Saint Helena. Surely Lord Crestor could take some time away from his duties to be here for the holidays?"

"You seem unduly concerned by his absence, Ellie." Selina raised her eyebrows as she looked at her maid.

"I'm the one who dried your tears after he left, my lady. I know how much you love him."

"Yes, well, Lord Crestor made it perfectly clear that any thoughts of affection I might have had were misplaced when he released me from any prior claim to him just before he left to join his regiment in April."

"My lady, you know that he hadn't formally asked for your hand. He wanted you to be free in case he should be killed in battle."

"We've been over this before, Ellie. He obviously didn't care for me as much as I did for him." Selina forced a smile upon her face and picked up the lighted taper on the bedside table. "Come, my mouth is watering when I think of the roasted quail and apple tarts that are taking up space in the larder this very moment."

They made their way down the stairs, through the darkened entryway, and tiptoed past the housekeeper's quarters at the back of the house until they reached the door leading to the kitchen. Selina put a shaky hand against the frame as a loud rumble of hunger emitted from her stomach once again. Without further ado, she turned the knob and entered the room.

"Selina…um, Lady Selina? Is that you?"

Her hand trembled, and the candle wavered as she heard the sound of the deep, soothing voice of the man she had known and loved since childhood. She raised the candle and focused her gaze on the figure that had risen from the nearby table. She stifled a gasp when she saw him clearly. He had lost a considerable amount of weight in the months since he had gone away to battle. His black hair was still thick and wavy, brushed back off his forehead. But his cheekbones seemed more pronounced and prominent on his face. He had taken off his coat and draped it over the back of a chair. His cravat was untied and his white linen shirt hung loosely across his chest. As she looked into his hazel eyes, she had the impression that he was holding himself in check—hiding something from her. "Robert? Uh, Lord Crestor? I thought you were still in Brussels."

"I was until a few weeks ago. I had some business in London to attend to for the past several days and didn't stop for a meal before I came here. Were you late arriving as well?"

"No, no. I found I was still hungry. I couldn't sleep." As if on cue, her stomach growled loudly. She put her hand over it in an attempt to quiet the noisy organ. It was at that moment she realized she was standing in front of Robert wearing only her nightclothes. Her hair was unbound, hanging loosely across her shoulders. She turned away from him. "Please finish your meal, my lord. I will return to my room."

"I protest, Lady Selina; it is obvious you need something to eat. I would be a heartless individual to turn you away. Please sit down and share the food with me. Look, I discovered some sliced beef, two roasted quail, and a large portion of boiled potatoes. There are also apple tarts for dessert."

She stared with barely concealed longing at the abundant amount of edible items covering the table.

"My lady, go on and have something. I'll sit over here on a chair in the corner and wait for you."

Selina had forgotten Ellie's presence after her shock at seeing Robert. She faced him again. "My lord, you remember my lady's maid Miss Eleanor Worth?"

Robert inclined his head. "How do you do, Miss Worth?"

Ellie beamed back at him and curtseyed. "I'm very well, thank you, my lord."

"Sit down, Lady Selina. I'll fetch you a plate and some utensils." Robert strode across the room and reached inside a cupboard.

Selina pulled her wrapper more tightly across her body before lowering herself onto a chair at the table. Her brilliant idea of locating some sustenance was quickly turning into an extremely embarrassing circumstance. "I don't need much, just something to tide me over until morning."

Robert sat across from her and began spooning some of the potatoes onto the plate. "What happened this evening? Didn't Cook fix enough food to go around?"

"No, no, Cook made a beautiful feast. There was plenty for everyone."

He placed a slice of beef and one of the quail next to the potatoes and then handed her the dish. He frowned at her. "I don't understand. Did you have travel sickness? I've never known you to suffer any ill effects from being cooped up in a carriage for hours on end."

Selina pursed her lips together and avoided his direct look. She picked up her fork and pierced a slice of beef. "It's…It's a fairly recent affliction. I…I get uncomfortable when I am required to eat in the presence of others who are not known to me."

He didn't say anything for a moment. Then he reached for his tankard and took a sip from it. "I must admit your confession astounds me. You say this is a recent occurrence. When was the first instance that you were discomposed while eating?"

"It all started at Almack's. I attended a ball there in

June." She took a bite of the beef and savored the rich, roasted flavors.

"Here, let me get you some ale." He got up and poured some of the golden liquid into a cup and placed it in front of her. "Go on."

She thanked him before continuing her story. "My mother and I stopped at the refreshment table to procure something to eat. I had just taken a bite of bread when Lady Jersey arrived and requested to be introduced to me."

Robert sat down again and picked up his fork. "Busy body woman; always poking her nose into other people's business!"

Selina frowned as she remembered more details of the fateful evening. "I wasn't bothered by her direct attitude. I knew I would have to meet all the patronesses at some point. The problem came about as I quickly swallowed the bread and curtseyed to the lady as my mother performed the introductions. When I stood and opened my mouth to speak, I choked on a crumb that was stuck in my throat. I began to cough uncontrollably."

Robert studied her. "I'm not surprised you came to grief. Everyone knows about the atrocious stale bread and dry cake that is served at Almack's. I wouldn't be at all surprised to hear many of its patrons have had difficulties similar to yours. However, such an occurrence shouldn't affect your eating habits indefinitely."

Selina looked away from him and took a drink from her cup. The ale was cool and refreshing with a subtle, tart taste. "I know it's silly of me, but I was very embarrassed at the time. Lady Jersey of all people! Now

I've got myself in a panic over such a thing happening again."

"You say this nervousness occurs when you are confronted with people you don't know. Surely everyone at the table tonight was known to you?"

"No, that's not true. Your mother invited a Lord Bartley and his two sisters and their friend Sir William Elsmere to spend the holidays here. Apparently the fairly recent death of the Bartley's parents in a carriage accident left them in an understandably less than celebratory state of mind. Lady Dunstable was a good friend of the late Lady Bartley in her youth. I understand she hopes to bring about a sort of consolation by including them in the holiday celebrations."

A loud snoring sound suddenly came from the corner of the room. Selina turned to see Ellie leaning back in her chair, arms folded across her chest, with her mouth wide open. "I had forgotten. She is very tired."

"And you're very hungry. She'll be fine where she is for a few more minutes."

Selina faced her plate once more and busied herself with the task of eating, thankful that she wasn't having any problems swallowing the tasty morsels with Robert sitting across from her. The quicker she could finish, the sooner she could rouse Ellie and escape to her room. She stabbed a boiled potato with her fork and dropped it into her mouth.

"Did you have an opportunity to dance with Justin at Almack's?"

Selina looked up and frowned at him in confusion as she swallowed a morsel of beef. "Justin?"

"My best friend and your acquaintance for many years, Justin Wexler, the Marquess of Rockton. Did you meet him there?"

"Oh." She sipped some more of the cool brew. "No, I didn't see him at Almack's."

"I didn't have time to correspond with him since I went away. And there was little chance of receiving a letter in Brussels because my location changed quite often."

"You will certainly have many opportunities to speak to him if you intend on staying here. He was also invited to spend the holidays at your parents' home. He was at dinner this evening." Selina cut a slice of meat from the roasted quail.

"Justin is here?" He stared at her with an arrested look on his face. "Of course, it would be hard to be parted over the holidays."

"Yes, I believe his aunt and his current heir, her son, decided to stay at their home in London for the Christmas holidays this year." Selina answered him in a crisp manner, confused by his preoccupation with Lord Rockton, albeit he was his valued friend. "I'm certain you will be able to learn all about his recent activities and the state of his health over breakfast tomorrow morning."

"Why don't you tell me something of his recent pursuits, Selina?"

She spooned the last of the potatoes into her mouth and glanced around the table.

"Did you say there were apple tarts?"

"Here." Robert turned and plucked one of the flaky pastries off a plate on the counter and placed it in front of her. "Well?"

She took a bite of the pastry and then closed her eyes to savor the tart, slightly sweet dessert as the bits of apple caressed her tongue. When she looked up a moment later, she started in surprise when she discovered Robert bent forward across the table, his pale, careworn face only a few inches from her own. "I...I'm sorry. Did you say something?"

"I...it's not important." He sat back down and leaned against the back of his chair. He studied his tankard of ale before reaching for it and taking a sip. "As you say, I can learn all I need to know from Justin in the morning."

Selina stood up and reached down to make sure her wrapper was secured. His presence in the room with her after so many months away at war was causing great havoc with her emotions. Memories of the pain and hurt she had experienced when Robert told her she should not wait for him were threatening to engulf her. At the same time, it was hard to see him so changed—a faded image of the likeness she kept in her subconscious as something to hold onto and treasure daily. She felt a sudden urge to wrap her arms around his lean shoulders and whisper comforting words in his ear. She must not tarry here any longer. "Thank...thank you for allowing me to share your meal. I'm very grateful."

He got up from his chair and walked around the table to stand next to her. He reached out to clasp her arm. "You know I would do anything for you, Selina."

She could feel the wet tears forming at the corners of her eyes. She hastily turned away from him before he noticed them and she said something she would regret later. She reached out to shake her maid's arm. "Ellie, Ellie, wake up. It's time for us to return to our beds."

Chapter Two

He dreamed of her that evening. She stood before him in a lush garden setting—tall rose bushes that were heavy with pink and white blossoms waved in the breeze behind her. Her green eyes, the color of a stormy sea, were focused on his face. She was speaking to him. Her full red lips were moving but he couldn't hear what she was saying. He reached out to tuck a lock of her long, silken black hair behind her ear. She backed away from him before he could touch her. Then she began to cry, the tears trickling slowly down her smooth, unblemished cheeks.

"No!" He opened his eyes, stared up at the darkened ceiling and realized he was in his bedchamber. He took several deep breaths to calm his wildly pounding heart as he tried to make sense of the nightmare. What had Selina been attempting to tell him? Why was she crying? He slept fitfully for what remained of the night, his thoughts in a state of great confusion.

He rose from his bed in the early morning. He was very tired after the disruptive, nearly sleepless night but he knew the habits of his friend Justin too well. He was one to break his fast not long after the sun had risen. He needed to confront him when he was alone. This would be a perfect opportunity to do so before the others joined them.

He had warned his valet of his intent the evening

before. Foxtel was waiting in the connecting room with a bowl full of warm water. He had a moment to note that his clothing for the morning was draped neatly on a nearby chair. Foxtel was a treasure. He had served in the war as a private and had come to Robert's notice when he observed his seemingly abundant energy and optimism even during the worst of the battles. His own valet had left to live permanently with his sister on the same day Robert had traveled to join the cavalry. When Foxtel had informed him he had no place to return to at war's end, he had offered him the position. Foxtel had adapted quickly to the duties of care and cleaning of his garments as well as proving himself an expert with a razor.

"Good morning, my lord. I trust you slept well?"

"Relatively well. Thank you, Foxtel."

"We'll have you ready in a trice, my lord. Please sit down."

A short time later, Robert emerged from his bedchamber immaculately clad in a bottle-green-colored frock coat over a gray waistcoat that was shot with silver thread. He had instructed Foxtel to tie his cravat in a casual manner that somehow came off looking elegant. His gray breeches were tucked into shiny leather Hessian boots. He was conscious that his garments hung very loosely on his slender frame but there had been no time to order new clothes during his short visit to London. He strode along the hallway, making his way quickly down the grand staircase. Huntley, the butler was at his post near the door. He bowed to Robert as he came near.

"Good morning, Lord Crestor. May I extend my warmest wishes for a wonderful Christmas and say how happy I am that you made it home for the holidays?"

"Good morning, Huntley. Thank you. My mother and father will certainly be in for a surprise when they see me."

"Lord and Lady Dunstable will be overjoyed, my lord. Cook has far surpassed herself this morning. You will find Lord Rockton inside the breakfast room."

"Thank you, Huntley." Robert walked down the hallway and entered the chamber.

"Robert! Good God! Is that you?"

He strode across the room and embraced his friend. "Yes, it is I, Justin. Many pounds lighter and with a rather dim, sobering view of the world at present, I'm afraid."

"I barely recognize you! You need to put some meat on those bones. Grab a plate and dig in. Cook has prepared a tremendous feast for us on this Christmas Eve morning."

Robert went over to the sideboard and studied the various dishes. There was bacon, grilled trout in white butter sauce, smoked herrings, and sausages with mashed potatoes. Several kinds of fresh breads and rolls overflowed from inside decorative baskets. Butter, honey, orange marmalade, and apple and cherry jam were in various dishes nearby. He helped himself to several items and then sat down across the table from Justin.

"Would you care for coffee or tea, my lord?" A servant suddenly appeared at his elbow with two silver jugs.

"Coffee please. That will be all for me for now."

Justin had his cup refilled before speaking. "How long has it been since you left Brussels?"

"Almost a month." He forked a sausage and dipped it in some mashed potatoes. "I stayed until Kilgore was well enough to travel home. You knew that Edward, Lord Kilgore was severely wounded at Waterloo?"

"Yes, I heard he almost lost a leg."

Robert took a bite of the sausage and then a sip of his coffee. "It was a near thing. The doctor wanted to take it off, but he was insistent that they leave him whole. Infection set in shortly after they removed the bullet from his leg—just below the knee. I stayed by his side during the raging depths of his fever and took it upon myself to clean the dressing twice daily even when he was thrashing about on the bed caught up in hallucinations brought on by the sickness. I was very relieved when his fever finally broke a few days later."

"It sounds as if he owes you his life."

Robert shrugged as he spooned a dollop of jam on a slice of bread. "As you can imagine, medical supplies were very meager with so many men wounded and needing attention. I was lucky enough to come out of the battles unscathed. It gave me a sense of purpose to help Kilgore and others who were not so fortunate."

"I must say I felt guilty that I couldn't join you."

Robert looked up from his plate and studied his friend. Unlike himself, Justin hadn't changed much over the last several months. He still wore his thick, golden-hued hair long, off his high forehead, tied back with a thin, black leather strap. Fine, sandy-colored brows and pronounced cheekbones framed large green eyes. A classic, aristocratic nose that was slightly bent at the bridge hovered over firm lips and a strong chin. "I'm glad your numerous responsibilities kept you at home. I don't think I could have withstood the pain and great sense of calamity I would have experienced if you had perished on the battlefield."

"How do you think I felt when news of the horrific loss of life at Waterloo reached me? I pored over the lists of names of the dead, holding my breath, wanting to believe you had survived but also realizing the sheer impossibility of it when I saw the number of men who were gone forever."

Robert sighed and pushed away his empty plate. A servant entered the room. He removed the dish and refilled the gentlemen's cups of coffee before leaving.

"As I said before, I was very fortunate to escape from that appalling battle unharmed." He drank some of the hot liquid and contemplated his friend intently. "What about you, Justin? What have you been doing with yourself while I was gone? Did you have a chance to visit London during the Season?"

"I spent some time in the city, mostly visiting my aunt and cousin, but you are quite familiar with the myriad number of responsibilities I have to deal with almost daily on my estate. Those duties make it hard for me to be away for any great length of time."

"You came to no understanding with a special woman?"

Justin paused as he was raising his cup to his lips. He lowered it back to the table, with a confused expression upon his face. "Did you suffer a severe blow to the head in battle? You of all people know that I do all I can to stay out of the parson's mousetrap. I have no interest in getting married for several years yet."

"I was under the impression that you had decided to change your plans for the immediate future and settle down."

Justin pushed his chair back and stood up from the table. "I can't possibly imagine what gave you such a silly notion. I know that I never told you that I was attracted to any special woman. Get another plate of food, Robert. Your loss of weight must be causing you to come up with some rather extreme flights of fancy."

****

"Be quick, Ellie. I want to be gone before Lord Crestor goes downstairs for breakfast." Selina gulped the rest of her hot chocolate and took a bite of toast. She strode across the room, turned with her back toward her maid, who was holding her coat. She struggled to get her arms inside the tight sleeves of the fur-lined pelisse.

"First you pick at your food at the dinner table and end up eating from the kitchen larder when you should have been in your bed. Now you neglect to do what is proper and partake of the morning meal with the others downstairs. It is Christmas Eve after all. I beg your pardon my lady, but I don't understand why you are acting this way."

"I know it's silly of me. How I wish I had never picked up that stale thing at Almack's! Now I have dwelled upon the incident and made myself awkward and discomfited. To add to my uneasiness, Robert, Lord Crestor makes a surprise appearance, and I find I am shamefully out of countenance."

"But my lady, you had no problem eating with him in the kitchen last night."

"You saw how he was, Ellie. He insisted I share the impromptu feast with him. My only thought at that time was to finish my meal as quickly as possible so that I could return to my bedchamber." She felt her face flush as she thought more about the incident. "How

131

mortifying that was to eat with him dressed only in my nightgown and flimsy wrapper!"

"I'm certain Lord Crestor wouldn't ever complain about the clothes you were wearing," her maid replied in a smug fashion.

"I feel I've suffered enough over the past few months after his casual abandonment of me. I had no wish to bring further complications by adding extremely embarrassing situations to the coil. That is precisely why I'm intent on avoiding the breakfast room and his company this morning. Come, let us go. A brisk walk on the grounds will do us both good."

"Yes, my lady." Ellie sounded quite unenthusiastic about the prospect.

Selina walked out of the bedchamber door and pulled on her gloves as she hurried down the stairs.

"Lady Selina, we are just going into breakfast. Won't you join us, or have you already eaten?"

Selina looked below to find Lord Bartley, Sir William, and the Bartley sisters clustered together in the hallway. The door to the library opened behind them and Justin, Lord Rockton emerged. "I have it on good authority that Lady Selina has not breakfasted as yet as I was the first to partake of only a tiny sampling of the tremendous amount of food Cook has produced for us. There is grilled trout with butter sauce, sausages with mashed potatoes, bacon, smoked herrings and baskets filled with fresh breads and rolls accompanied by delicious jams and orange marmalade. You can't mean to skip such a feast, my dear?"

Selina could feel her stomach begin to clench as she listened to Lord Rockton's mouthwatering descriptions. Ellie wasn't helping the situation—standing next to her with her eyebrows raised on her forehead, nodding in the direction of the breakfast room.

"I intended to take a walk around the gardens before eating."

"Walking was a favorite pastime of our mother's," the elder Miss Bartley spoke softly with a solemn expression on her face. "It would bring me much pleasure to accompany you after breakfast."

"Oh yes, could I come as well?" the younger Frances Bartley pleaded.

Selina forced a smile onto her face as she saw Lord Rockton winking and nodding at her from his place at the back of the group. "I would appreciate your companionship, ladies. I suppose I could eat something now."

"Wonderful. Lead the way, Lady Selina." Lord Bartley stepped back to allow her to precede him.

Huntley was waiting for them, and he opened the breakfast room door with a flourish. "Enjoy your meal, my lords and ladies!"

Selina walked into the room and immediately wished she had stuck to her original plan when she spotted Robert talking with her mother and father as they piled their plates with food. His parents were standing nearby beaming at him with obvious pride.

"Selina! We were just speaking of you." Lady Burford put her plate down on the table and stepped toward her. "Happy Christmas Eve, dear."

Selina gave her a quick kiss on the cheek. "The same to you, Mother. What were you talking about?"

"I was only asking Robert if he had seen you since he arrived last evening." Her mother lowered her voice to a whisper. "Such a surprise he has given us all. A wonderful Christmas present to Andrew and Louisa!"

"Yes, to have him here for the holidays after the many anxious months while he was away must be very gratifying for them both."

"How are you holding up, Selina?"

"I'm fine, Mother. It is a shock to see him so thin, but I'm sure Cook will fatten him up very quickly if she continues to produce such delicious meals as this breakfast and the dinner we had last night."

"Happy holidays, my dear." Her father walked up and hugged her. "We were becoming concerned when we didn't find you at the table."

Selina returned his embrace. "Yes, well, I had planned to go walking first, but the Misses Bartley convinced me to have my meal now so that they may join me on a stroll when we have finished."

She greeted Robert's parents, Lord and Lady Dunstable before turning to peruse the nearby sideboard that was covered with dishes of food. Selina sniffed the air appreciatively.

"Were you attempting to skip breakfast as well?" She heard the whispered voice and discovered Robert standing next to her.

"Certainly not, I planned to eat later. You heard me mention to my father I was about to set out for a walk but postponed my plans at the request of the Bartleys."

"I didn't tell your mother about our chance meeting in the kitchen."

"Thank you for not saying anything about it." She moved away from him and picked up a plate.

She found him at her elbow once again. "Of course you are well aware that Justin breaks his fast quite early in the morning. There was little chance you would be ready at that time."

"I have no idea what you are talking about, my lord. I have absolutely no clue why I should be interested in Lord Rockton's eating habits."

"Quit dawdling, Lady Selina. Everyone else has filled their plates. I've even gone back for seconds. Come and join us." Lord Rockton's voice rang out over everyone else's happy chatter and the sound of cutlery clanging against the white porcelain dishes.

"His first thought should be of your welfare." Robert muttered before moving away and joining his parents at the table.

Selina frowned in confusion at his words. What could he be referring to? He seemed greatly changed by his experiences on the battlefield. She hoped it was only a temporary predicament. She shrugged her shoulders as she reminded herself that Robert didn't wish for her to have any type of interference in his life. It was up to his family to concern themselves with his health and welfare. She turned and faced the many delicacies on the sideboard. After making several selections from the dishes and baskets, she sat at the empty chair between her mother and Lord Rockton.

A servant appeared at her side and poured her tea. She added milk and sugar and sipped the hot beverage with a sigh of relief.

"Lady Dunstable's cook has excelled herself this morning. The meal last night was delicious as well." Lord Rockton took a bite of trout.

"Indeed. The cook, a Mrs. Morton, is of the third generation in her family to dignify the kitchens of this estate." Selina's mother took a drink of her tea. "I understand that many of the recipes were originally concocted by Mrs. Morton's grandmother."

Selina glanced over at the crowded sideboard where a servant was adding more slices of bacon to a half-empty dish. "Cook is obviously quite comfortable preparing an abundant selection of food."

"I can only imagine the banquet she has planned for us tonight." Lord Rockton forked the last bit of sausage into his mouth and pushed his chair away from the table. "No more food for me. Lady Selina, you have hardly touched your breakfast."

Since sitting down at the table, Selina had been conscious of Robert's intense gaze upon her face. She had attempted to ignore him but couldn't stop herself from glancing at him from time to time. Her preoccupation with him had caused her to forget about her food. She picked up her fork and grinned up at Lord Rockton. "I was so busy admiring the feast that I forgot to taste it as well."

"You're not suffering an attack of nerves again, my dear?" her mother whispered in her ear.

"No, don't worry, Mother." She bit into a piece of bacon and then picked up a slice of the warm bread. She spooned some of the orange marmalade onto the surface.

"If I may invite myself, I'd like to join you and the others on your walk, Lady Selina." Lord Rockton stood up from his chair and bowed to her.

"Of course you may come, my lord."

"I trust my presence on the outing as well will not cause any awkwardness?"

Selina noticed Robert had moved to stand just behind Lord Rockton. "Whatever can you mean, Lord Crestor? You are certainly welcome to come with us."

"There is Bartley and Sir William, and a sister each

for them. Then there is you and Justin. I am decidedly the odd man out on this excursion."

Selina frowned when she heard Robert couple her with Lord Rockton. She remembered his veiled expression when she had first come upon him in the kitchen last night and his assumption later that she would know all about his friend's recent activities. Surely he didn't believe…

"You young people enjoy yourselves. Perhaps you can collect some greenery while you are out as well. I'm sure Louisa would appreciate it. There never seems to be quite enough to decorate such a large house as this is." Her mother didn't appear to notice anything amiss with Robert's comments.

"Let's leave Lady Selina to finish her meal in peace. We'll meet in the entryway in half an hour if that is acceptable to you, my dear?"

Selina didn't think she was imagining it, but she thought she saw Robert flinch when Lord Rockton spoke the words of affection to her. Was he suffering from some type of hidden injury he had received in battle? "Are you well, Lord Crestor?"

He raised his eyebrows when she asked the question. "Yes, I am fine."

"He's suffering from lack of nourishment. With Cook's help he should be well on the way to recovery before too many days have passed." Lord Rockton spoke in a sarcastic manner as he glared at his friend. He turned back to Selina. "Is thirty minutes acceptable?"

"That is perfectly acceptable, my lord."

Chapter Three

Robert took a sip from his glass of brandy and stared at the glowing flames in the fireplace. He mulled over the events that had occurred on the late morning walk. With one exception, the excursion had been quite civilized—mostly devoid of any drama or tension. The Bartley sisters had strolled in front with Lady Selina while he had joined Lord Bartley, Sir William, and Justin bringing up the rear of the group.

The discussions they had together during the outing had been commonplace, even mundane. Lord Bartley had commented on the vastness of the Dunstable estate. He had requested advice about the best methods to implement crop rotation on his own property. This was a subject near and dear to Justin and the two gentlemen had debated the issue for most of the trek. Sir William had asked Robert for his own impressions of the city of Brussels before the horrific battle of Waterloo had begun.

The women talked in low, soft voices to one another. He had heard fragments of their conversations. Selina had commented on the brisk, cold wind as they reached the summit of the pathway that bordered the estate. The elder Miss Bartley had asked her if it ever snowed during the winter in this area. At her affirmative answer, the younger Bartley sister had giggled and clapped her hands, seemingly in hopes of catching a glimpse of some white globs of ice before the holiday was over.

Just before they had reached the courtyard that would lead them back into the house, Huntley appeared bearing two cloth sacks. "My lords, Sir William, Lady Selina and Misses Bartley, Lady Dunstable has requested that you gather a few branches of greenery to decorate the dinner table and sitting room. When you return, hot chocolate and butter shortbread will be waiting for you."

A chorus of "oohs" and "aahs" broke out from the group.

"How about having some sherry for the ladies and brandy for the gentlemen on hand as well, Huntley?" Robert clasped his gloved hands together and blew on them. It was getting colder as the morning moved on toward afternoon.

"Of course, my lord."

Sir William and Justin each took a bag. Lord Bartley and his sisters joined forces with Justin. Robert found himself accompanying Selina and Sir William on their quest for bits of holly and pine branches.

A thick, natural wooded area was close by, not too far off the path. Robert led the way and soon the two groups had split apart, each concentrating on collecting greenery from what they considered to be the best specimens. Sir William found a bushy pine tree, and he began cutting some of the lower branches using a small knife that he pulled from his pocket.

Selina wandered toward a holly bush that had entangled itself around the trunk of a large birch tree. She started pulling on one of the branches that had a cluster of red berries upon it.

"Let me help you." Robert rushed over to Selina imagining the sharp thorns on the leaves piercing her thin leather gloves and stabbing her soft, tender skin. He pulled a small pair of scissors from his waistcoat pocket.

"Thank you. I'm glad to see you came prepared."

"My valet, Foxtel gave these to me recently. It is amazing how often I have had occasions to need scissors since that time. I don't know what I ever did without them." Robert realized he was chattering inanely. Selina must think he'd gone daft after his sobering experiences in battle.

"There are quite a few branches with berries on them. The dinner table will look very festive this evening." She sounded nervous, uncomfortable with their conversation.

"I certainly hope you will be able to do justice to the feast that Cook is preparing for us." As soon as the words were out of his mouth, Robert regretted them. There was nothing like pointing out a person's weakness to them—a sure way of gaining their scorn. He never, ever intended for Selina to despise him. The thought of losing her friendship suddenly made it difficult for him to breathe.

"You needn't concern yourself, my lord. But I…I am hopeful that my uneasiness has passed. I did very well at breakfast this morning."

It was just as he had feared. Her tone of voice sounded tense and angry when she answered him. He must attempt to make amends. "I'm sorry. I spoke without thinking, and I have embarrassed you. You must believe that was not my intention. I was concerned about your welfare."

"Must I remind you that your anxiety over my well-being is misplaced, my lord? You set me free, remember? The state of my health can be no concern of yours."

Robert was shocked by Selina's cold, hostile manner. He opened his mouth to protest her assumptions only to be interrupted by Sir William.

"Lord Crestor, you're wasting a golden opportunity."

Frustrated by the disruption, Robert turned toward the gentleman, aware that his expression mirrored the ill-temper and indignation that was churning inside him. "What are you talking about?"

Sir William stepped backward and dropped his half-filled bag to the ground. "I...I, the mistletoe, it's... hanging above your heads."

Robert twisted around and spied the cluster of yellowish green leaves decorated with white berries hanging over them, clinging to one side of the trunk. He stepped away from the tree just as he heard the voices of the others.

"We have our bag filled," called out one of the Bartley sisters. "Do you need our assistance?"

"What, ho! You two found some mistletoe!" Lord Bartley declared loudly.

Out of the corner of his eye, Robert had seen Selina compress her lips together and stare down at the ground. She was undoubtedly as discomfited by the situation as he was. He remembered thinking that he must act quickly to get them out of this coil. "No. You don't understand. We never saw it."

Justin had scowled at him from his position behind Lord Bartley. "Did I hear you correctly? No?"

"I'll gladly do the honors." Lord Bartley then

stepped forward, put his hands on Selina's shoulders, and bent over to kiss her cheek.

The Bartley sisters had giggled, Selina flushed and looked uncomfortable. Lord Bartley seemed quite pleased with himself.

The group swiftly dispersed at that point. Lord Bartley escorted Selina and his sisters into the house. Robert had accompanied Sir William, who babbled nervously about the upcoming Christmas Eve dinner and Justin, stone-faced, and silent strode over to the servants' entrance where he left the bags of pine and holly branches with a servant.

Robert stretched his legs out in front of him and took another sip of brandy. He wasn't feeling sociable. He assumed the others had gathered in the sitting room for beverages and shortbread. The unsettling dream he had last night combined with the disconcerting events that occurred today had left him decidedly confused and perplexed. He stared at the dancing flames.

"Are you planning on joining the rest of us, son?" his father's voice rang out from the doorway.

He came to his feet and raised his glass. "No, I'll just finish this drink and head to my room to change for dinner."

"I know this is your first full day back home after the ghastly experiences I'm certain you faced on the battlefield. I hesitate to say anything. But you must make amends with Lady Selina as quickly as possible."

Robert frowned at his father. "What do you mean?"

"Your mother and I are aware that you did what you deemed the honorable thing to do and told Lady Selina that she was free before you left, but now that you have returned in one piece, thank goodness, you need to reinstate your intentions to her."

"Other circumstances have come to my attention that make such a thing impossible to do."

"You're talking in riddles. Explain yourself."

"To be clear, she is in love with someone else."

"What? I don't believe it! Did she tell you this?"

"She didn't need to say anything to me. I saw the evidence with my own eyes. I don't wish to say any more on the subject."

His father sighed and turned away from him. "I wish you would verify her true feelings. I sense you are reading the situation incorrectly."

****

Selina reached up with a shaking hand to touch the strand of white pearls at her neck as she made her way downstairs. She still hadn't recovered from the embarrassing situation earlier in the day with Robert and the mistletoe. Thankfully, he didn't join them for tea and biscuits this afternoon. How was she to face him now? The delicious Christmas Eve feast Cook had surely prepared was going to taste like dry bread crumbs in her mouth if she managed to take any bites at all. If it had been any other night, she would have requested her meal be sent up on a tray to her room.

Justin, Lord Rockton, was standing by himself in the entry. He seemed to be deeply absorbed in contemplating the arrangement of the tiles on the floor. He looked up and smiled at her as she reached the bottom step.

"Ah, Lady Selina, you look beautiful. That dark shade of green makes your eyes glow like jewels and your hair shine like silk."

Gracious! She had known him for many years but

couldn't remember him speaking to her in such a devoted, charming manner. She hastily looked down at her dress. Her confused thoughts about Robert and his actions had caused her to be distracted when Ellie helped her into her garments. She had barely glanced in the mirror before she left her room. "Thank you so much for your compliments, my lord. This dress is a particular favorite of mine."

He reached down to clasp her hand. "Let me assure you the lady wearing the dress makes the garment that much more beautiful. I doubt that many other women in my acquaintance could do such a thing, my dear."

"You're very kind."

"I wish to ask you something. You and I have known Robert for many years." He squeezed her hand and she looked into his face to find him staring at her intently. "I'm concerned about his behavior. He made some strange comments to me at breakfast that made me angry. I held my temper in check at the time thinking that he needed the opportunity to readjust to life away from the battlefield. But his almost blatant refusal to embrace you under the mistletoe this morning has me very confused. Do have any explanation for his demeanor? Have the two of you quarreled?"

Selina took a deep breath before answering. "Robert...Lord Crestor set me free before he left to join the cavalry. He doesn't wish to marry me."

"Set you free...?" Lord Rockton frowned and seemed confused.

"He told me that since nothing had been made official we needn't consider ourselves betrothed."

Lord Rockton turned away from her, not speaking for several seconds. "This is a fine kettle of fish.

Whatever can he have been thinking? Ever the honorable, all-that-is proper gentleman, I suppose."

"I…I hesitate to presume, my lord, but some of the things he has said…" Selina stopped herself reluctant to mention her dubious assumptions.

"Well? Go on."

"I think it could be possible Robert believes you and me…"

"What?" He looked down at her with an arrested expression. Suddenly a grin lit up his face with mirth and he began to chuckle. He took her hand and placed it on top of his arm. "I was perplexed when he questioned me about how often I had visited London and even more astonished when he asked if I had a special woman in my life. Now his queries make sense."

"You believe my hunch is correct?"

"I think it's as safe as the bank." He paused and looked thoughtful. "I can imagine you have suffered greatly over the past few months. It must have been very hard for you. I know how much you love him."

"Goodness, I had no idea my feelings showed that clearly."

"It's not obvious, but I have known both of you for a long time. I've watched as your regard for Robert grew from adoration to affection and finally, true love. We're going to make the best of this situation and have some fun tonight, just follow my lead. The others have gathered in the drawing room to admire the festive decorations and to drink a toast to the holiday season. Let's join them."

Chapter Four

Robert couldn't stop himself from frowning as Justin entered the room with Selina on his arm. He stood very close to her, bending over to hear something she said. He chuckled and deftly squeezed her hand before leading her across the floor to join their group.

"Ah, perfect timing." His father indicated a tray that had two filled champagne glasses on it. "Help yourselves to the champagne."

"Here you are, my dear." Justin handed Selina a glass and then whispered something in her ear.

Robert saw Selina nod her head in acknowledgement of whatever sweet nothings Justin had certainly spoken to her. Then she turned away to face the others.

He took the opportunity to move closer to her. "I see that everything is as it should be. You two made quite a grand entrance."

"Happy holidays, my lord." Selina answered him with a cool, emotionless tone.

"I want to wish all of you a wonderful holiday season and hope you will enjoy your time here with us," his father's voice boomed out. "My wife and I also want our son Robert to know how proud we are of him and his service to our country. And how very grateful we are that he is home to spend Christmas with us."

He was surrounded by happy, smiling faces and

then a resounding chorus of hurrahs. Feeling somewhat overwhelmed, he raised his glass. "Thank you, Father and Mother. Thank you all. I am very happy to be back in one piece. Happy Christmas!"

His mother placed her glass on a nearby table and clapped her hands for attention. "Before dinner is served, Miss Bartley has graciously offered to play a few songs on the pianoforte for our pleasure. Miss Frances Bartley will also sing a tune."

Cheering and murmurs of approval broke out as both sisters' faces turned a rosy hue.

"I am certain you have discovered for yourselves, we are most fortunate in our cook, Mrs. Morton. She and I have worked tirelessly over the past few weeks discussing menus and various dishes. Please do your best to do justice to the tremendous feast we will be served tonight. Now enjoy the music."

After placing their empty glasses on the tray, everyone moved toward the group of chairs that had been placed on the other side of the room facing the pianoforte. Lord and Lady Burford sat at the front next to his father and mother. Selina, with her hand still clutching Justin's forearm moved to a chair behind her parents. Justin quickly claimed the seat next to her. Lord Bartley choose the empty chair next to Lady Burford and Sir William settled himself on Justin's other side. Robert found himself taking the only remaining unoccupied chair beside Selina.

"It was always a tradition in our home to play and sing songs on Christmas Eve," announced the elder Miss Bartley. "We hope you enjoy the sonatas we have chosen to perform."

She began to play a pretty melody that Robert

quickly recognized as Mozart. Her sister stood by her side, hands folded in front of her, obviously waiting for her cue to sing. Robert closed his eyes, willing himself to relax and enjoy the music.

"Your hand...I'm sorry. You're so thin."

Selina's softly spoken comment in his ear jolted him upright in his seat. "Uh...I know. As you might guess, there wasn't much chance to sit at a table and eat proper meals."

"Was...was it terrible? The horrors you must have experienced. I apologize. I'm interrupting your obvious enjoyment of the performance. But I see Lord Bartley discussing something with my mother, and I thought I would speak to you. There are so few chances to talk together."

"Let me just say that I fear it will be many months before I will be able to close my eyes at night and not see maimed, bloodied bodies of countless young men or hear their deafening cries of distress and agony in my ears."

Selina gasped. "I...I can't imagine. I...I suppose I don't really want to."

"I'm very sorry. I spoke without thinking of your tender sensibilities." He twisted around in his chair to face her.

"No, no. I wanted to hear this. I wanted to know something of your experiences over the past few months." She looked directly at him for a moment and then abruptly stared down at the floor. "I thought of you every day. You must have realized when you set me free that it wouldn't stop me from being concerned about your welfare."

"It's good to know I was in your thoughts." He

glanced pointedly at her hand that was still wrapped around Justin's sleeve. "I believe I took for granted you would be preoccupied with other relationships in your life."

"Excellent performance, wasn't it, my dear?" Justin spoke out, effectively ending their tête-à-tête.

"Ah…ah, yes. Miss Bartley plays the pianoforte with great skill."

"It appears we will have a sampling of Miss Frances's voice next."

"Excuse me." Robert stood up from his chair to walk over and stand next to Miss Bartley. The emotional turmoil he was going through watching Selina with Justin, hearing her speak of her concern for his welfare, the sweet sound of her voice in his ear, was making him feel bird-witted. He needed a distraction. "Let me turn the pages of the music for you."

"Thank you, my lord."

He managed to keep his gaze fixed upon Miss Bartley's fingers as they tapped out the melodies of the next two songs. He could feel himself breathing a little easier as the Bartley sisters came to the end of their performance.

"That was wonderful, ladies. Thank you so much." His mother came to her feet. "We have a few minutes at our leisure before dinner will be served."

Robert walked over to one of the windows and stared at the bleak, winter landscape outside. Quite a contrast to what he had known in Brussels not many months ago.

"I hope you're prepared to stuff yourself tonight."

He turned around. Justin and Selina were standing together not far away from him. The others had left the room.

"I'm certainly hungry." Robert wasn't sure how to answer Justin's statement.

"Good. We can't have you blowing away in the harsh winter winds, which will happen if you don't get your appetite back."

"Thank you for your concern." Robert couldn't keep the sarcastic tone out of his voice when he answered him.

"Should we be going?" Selina didn't look at him. She appeared uncomfortable with their conversation.

"After you, my dear." Justin bowed gallantly and waved his hand with a flourish. "Coming, Robert?"

"In a moment." He turned back to the window, this time not really looking at the garden.

"I wanted to make certain you understood how extremely relieved and comforted I am by your safe return to England."

He twisted around at the sound of Selina's voice. She was standing just inside the half-opened doorway.

"Uh…thank you. I'll do my best to justify those feelings."

"Always take care of yourself. Knowing you are healthy and happy would bring me the greatest satisfaction."

****

Selina entered the dining room a few minutes later. Lord Rockton was at her side. Her hands were shaking and her heart was pounding so hard that she could feel the throbbing sensation inside her eardrums. She was not sorry she had spoken. In the short amount of time available to her, she knew she had to make Robert understand something of the pain he had caused her. Just as she should be aware of a small part of what he had experienced, no matter appalling the reality of it was for her to hear.

She took a deep breath in an effort to relax herself as she forced herself to take note of the sparkling glasses, glowing white china plates, and shiny, polished silverware, all framed by festive pieces of holly and pine branches. A massive crystal chandelier glimmered brightly with many candles as it hung from the ceiling, high above the table.

"Lord Rockton, Lady Selina, you two are seated here on this side. Lord Bartley, you are next to Lady Selina. Miss Frances, you are at this chair between Lord Burford and Lord Rockton. Miss Bartley, you will be here, to my right since the numbers are a little off and we are short one gentleman to make it even. Robert, you will be next to her and to your right will be Lady Burford." Lady Dunstable stood at her place at the foot of the table. "I trust everyone is comfortable and ready to eat?"

A chorus of affirmatives answered her query.

"Huntley, you may begin to serve our dinner."

"Yes, my lady."

Selina glanced across the table at Robert. He was listening to something her mother was commenting upon and had his head turned away from her.

"I confess I'm eager to see what the soup will be." Lord Rockton sounded ready to relish the meal from start to finish.

"Whatever it is, I'm certain it will be delicious." Selina mentally prepared herself to remain calm and enjoy the special banquet.

"My lords and ladies, the potato soup is served."

Huntley made the pronouncement with a grand flourish. Several footmen entered the room behind him. Each man carried a tray containing two bowls of steaming hot soup. The dishes were quickly passed around as Huntley opened bottles of red wine. He poured a small amount of the liquid into Lord Dunstable's glass. He took a sip and pronounced it excellent. The other glasses were filled while the footmen brought out baskets of freshly baked rolls and bread.

Lord Dunstable came to his feet and raised his glass. "Happy Christmas to us all!"

A chorus of jubilant assents answered his toast and then all was suddenly quiet except for the occasional clink of a spoon nudging the side of a bowl as everyone enjoyed their soup.

Selina closed her eyes and savored the flavors. The creamy, buttery broth with a hint of lemon paired with chunks of tender potatoes and bits of celery was excellent.

Lord Rockton lowered his spoon and sat back in his chair. "You were right. I've never tasted anything so delightful."

Huntley entered the room with great formality carrying a large, gaily decorated bowl with a lid on top. Two footmen followed behind him—one carried a tray of cups and the other had a large ladle in his hand.

"My lords and ladies, the Wassail Bowl."

"Capital!" Lord Bartley sat up straighter in his chair next to her. "It's been a long time since I had that punch."

Selina wasn't familiar with the drink. "Do you know what it's made of?"

"To my understanding it usually contains rum,

brandy and port—the juice of oranges and lemons with their rinds and sugar."

Lord Rockton leaned closer to her. "It's served warm as well. Sip it slowly, my dear. It's quite a potent beverage."

"With so much liquor in it, I'm not surprised to hear that, my lord."

"Many an unsuspecting gentleman has woken up Christmas morning with a dry mouth and a sore head after too many glasses of Wassail, I can tell you." Lord Bartley appeared well-acquainted with the drink.

Huntley ladled out small portions of the beverage into the cups and passed them around while the soup bowls were taken away.

Lord Rockton picked up his cup and turned to Selina. "Try a bit, my dear."

She took a taste and savored the warm, fruity Wassail. Then a sensation of dizziness suddenly hit her as the strong liquor entered her stomach. She hastily placed the cup back on the table. "The flavor is very good, but I can feel the effects of the rum, brandy and port almost immediately."

"I warned you it was strong."

The door opened again and Huntley entered bearing a large tray. He placed the platter in front of Lord Dunstable. "My lord, I give you the Christmas goose."

Lord Dunstable took the knife Huntley handed him and began to carve slices of meat off the large, roasted bird. While he was occupied in this task, Huntley directed the footmen as to the placement of assorted dishes and trays. Selina had a bowl of boiled potatoes put in front of her. Sliced roast beef was placed in front of Lady Dunstable. A dish of squash, a bowl of stuffing, a tray of oysters and an assortment of turnips, beets and lettuces completed the special meal.

Huntley stood at Lord Dunstable's side holding up empty plates. The earl dropped slices of the goose onto them. The footmen distributed the dishes around the table. The other items were passed between themselves.

Selina spooned a bit of squash before giving Lord Rockton the bowl. She took a deep breath and picked up her fork, telling herself to remain relaxed so she could enjoy the food that covered her plate.

"I say, Huntley, another cup of punch for me."

"Yes, my lord."

With a sensation of alarm, Selina looked over and noticed that Lord Bartley had gulped down his first serving of the Wassail in record time. She had a sudden, distressing image of him abruptly slipping from his seat at the table to land in an intoxicated pile at her feet. Just as quickly, she told herself not to be concerned. He was a peer of the realm, no longer a lad who was wet behind the ears. He should know how to handle his liquor.

For several minutes, no one spoke. It seemed everyone was enjoying their meal. Selina ate slowly and carefully, managing to swallow a tiny amount of her food.

"More of that Wassail, my good man!"

Selina became very anxious as she heard Lord Bartley's second request for punch. She dropped her fork onto her plate and gripped the serviette that covered her lap with stiff, shaking fingers.

"Are you certain?" Sir William spoke up from his chair.

"Go easy, Bartley." It seemed Lord Rockton was concerned as well.

154

Lord Bartley ignored both comments. He drank deeply from his newly replenished cup. "Lord Crestor, now that your days on the battlefield are over, I imagine you'll see to your own estate, probably settle down and get married, huh?"

Selina studied Robert for the second time since they had sat down. He looked up from his plate when he heard the question with an expression of surprise on his face. Then he glanced at her and cleared his throat. "You're correct. I have much to keep me busy after several months away from home."

"Avoiding the question? You're a downy one." Lord Bartley paused to take another drink. "I'm acquainted with several lovely, eligible ladies who would jump at the chance to entertain your suit— wealthy lord and war hero that you are. We can discuss their names later if you wish."

"Please, Brother! Remember where you are," Miss Bartley whispered from across the table.

Selina knew she couldn't sit in this room any longer. Her head was beginning to throb and her stomach felt as if it was tied in knots. She came to feet, tossing the serviette onto her chair. "I'm sorry. I'm not feeling well. I must go to my room."

Lord Rockton came to his feet beside her. "I will help you to your bedchamber, my dear."

"No, thank you, my lord. I will see to my daughter. Come along, dear."

Selina grasped her mother's arm with a grateful sigh. She couldn't help glancing over at Robert, noting his distressed expression as she turned toward the door.

Chapter Five

Robert balanced his candle in one hand and pushed open the door to the library without knocking. He quickly spotted Justin reclining on a chair near the fire with a glass of brandy beside him. He was idly turning the pages of a large book.

"You've heard that Selina is doing much better?" He put the candle on the mantel.

"Yes, her mother informed me that she was resting quietly in her room."

"Am I to wish you happy?"

Justin didn't speak. He closed the book with one swift movement, causing the pages to snap together. He reached for his brandy and took a drink before slowly lowering it to the table once more.

"Well?" What little patience Robert had at that moment was wearing thin.

"Excellent dinner we had this evening. Don't you agree?"

"I asked you a question."

"I thought I responded in a roundabout fashion. I'm happily satisfied and full after such a delicious feast."

"Quit evading the issue, Justin. Are you and Selina getting married?"

He draped one arm over the chair and reached for his glass once again.

"Dammit! Answer me!"

Infuriatingly, Justin sipped some brandy before turning to him. "Robert, you and I have been friends for a long time. Don't you think you would be one of the first to know if I had plans to take a wife?"

"Yes, of course I believe that. But in this instance, I suppose I thought you were saving the news until after the holidays or waiting a few weeks to tell me after I became acclimated to life without the cavalry or some such nonsense."

"The idea never crossed that thick skull of yours that Selina is and always has been in love with you?"

"In love with me?" His heart began to race, and he suddenly felt lightheaded. He forced himself to remain calm and to focus on the quandary at hand. "That isn't possible. I saw you both at Lord and Lady Toller's ball, the night before I left. You were gazing into each other's eyes."

Justin glared at him. "Please don't tell me you released her based solely on that instance."

"The thought of her alone if I should die played a part. But yes, I believed you two cared deeply for each other."

"Of course there is affection between us. I've known Selina almost as long as I've known you. That is exactly why I assured her the night of the Toller's ball that she could call on me while you were away for anything she might need. She was very grateful for my offer and thanked me profusely. Now you know what was going on when you saw us."

He didn't speak for a moment. The thought of his foolish assumptions that had bedeviled and tormented him for so many months made him want to kick himself. His father had warned him he could have misread the situation. He paced back and forth in frustration staring down at the floor.

"Wait!" He came to a sudden stop. "You two have smelled of April and May all night. You can't deny you were playing the part of her swain this evening."

Justin grinned at him. "I had a chance to question Selina earlier about your strange behavior. She hesitated to say anything to me at first, but eventually she admitted that some of the comments you had made to her caused her to believe you assumed we were in love. I decided to play up to your silly conjectures hoping that I could make you angry or jealous enough to finally recognize your love for Selina. It seems to have worked."

"You appear to know all about my true feelings. Did you say anything about my love for her when you were planning this escapade?"

"I would never mention such a thing to her. That is a private matter to be resolved between you and Selina. But I must warn you, she believes you don't love her."

"What? How can she believe such a thing? I have done nothing but attempt to conceal my affection for her since the moment I thought I realized she was in love with you. I did it all for her happiness."

"You assumed that we were in love, and you set free the woman who cared deeply for you without questioning what you saw. I believe you have broken her heart, Robert."

"No! I can't bear it. I couldn't have done such a thing!" He pounded his clenched fist into the palm of his hand in an attempt to relieve the anguish he was experiencing at the thought of the pain he had unknowingly caused her. "I must speak to her immediately."

"It's close to midnight. She's in her bed. You can't see her now."

"There must be some way." He was silent as he tried to think of a way to explain himself to her. There had been no chance for any discussion when she had suddenly left the table at dinner. "Wait... I think I have thought of an answer to my dilemma."

"Don't do anything rash."

He strode across the floor, grabbed his candle and yanked open the door. "I assure you, it's one of the most rational ideas I've had in a long time."

He raced down the hallway to the kitchen, hoping he hadn't missed his chance. He pushed open the door and found the room dark and empty. Pots and pans were stacked neatly on the shelves. Damp dish cloths hung out to dry on hooks near the stove. He glanced over at the table where he and Selina had shared their impromptu meal the night before. The surface was clean, the chairs pushed in underneath it.

"Lord Crestor, um...I'm sorry. Excuse me for disturbing you, my lord."

He turned and discovered Selina's maid standing in the doorway wearing her nightclothes. She reached up in a nervous manner to adjust the frilly, lace cap she wore on top of her head.

"Miss Worth. I can guess your errand. Your mistress doesn't join you?"

"No, not tonight, my lord. She is somewhat disturbed by the goings-on this evening at dinner. She asked that I bring the food straight to her bedchamber."

"I must ask a great favor of you, Miss Worth."

"What is it, my lord?"

"I wish to accompany you back to Lady Selina's room."

The maid raised her eyebrows when she heard his request. "That wouldn't be proper, my lord."

"Come now, Miss Worth, your presence will deem the situation more or less respectable."

"I…I don't know, my lord. Lady Selina is wearing her nightgown."

"That is nothing that I haven't already seen before. Please understand me, Miss Worth. Your mistress became upset earlier this evening partly because of a misunderstanding caused by my foolish assumptions. I need a chance to explain myself to her."

"I would be very grateful if you could make Lady Selina truly happy again, my lord. She has suffered mightily these past months."

"I intend to relieve her distress as quickly as possible. I'll help you fetch the food."

Miss Worth got a plate and some cutlery while he went to the larder. She held out the dish to him and he filled it with two slices of beef, a bit of goose, stuffing, potatoes, a roll and a piece of gingerbread for dessert.

"If you can carry that, I'll bring a glass and some ale. Lead the way."

Holding his candle high to guide them through the entryway and up the stairs, the maid came to a stop at a door a short way down the hall.

"What now, my lord?" she whispered.

He thought for a moment. He was extremely anxious to speak to Selina but it wouldn't do to startle her, cause her to scream in surprise or to make a loud noise, which would certainly bring others to her room who were most unwelcome at this time.

"Go inside with the food. Tell her that I'm waiting outside her door. All I'm asking for is a few minutes to explain myself to her with you in attendance."

"As you wish, my lord." She opened the door and quickly stepped inside, shutting it with a snap.

Robert balanced the glass and the jug of ale in one hand and gripped his candle in the other as he paced back and forth on the carpet in front of Selina's room. He could discern the sound of voices through the door. His heart began to race as he thought of the possibility that she would refuse to see him. She must give him a chance to speak to her.

The door suddenly clicked open. "Come in, my lord."

He stepped inside and immediately searched the interior for Selina. He quickly spotted her sitting at a small table that was placed near the fireplace. The plate of food was in front of her. She was wearing the same wrapper from the night before. Her hair had been gathered up to the crown of her head in haste. Several strands were even now coming loose and falling about her shoulders. He stared at the vision of loveliness before him.

"You wished to speak to me?"

Her soft voice recalled him to his purpose.

"Ah, yes, I do. Here…here is a glass and some ale." He put his candle on the table as well. "I wished to say that I discovered only minutes ago that I had done you a great disservice when I set you free before I left to join the cavalry."

"What did you discover, my lord?"

"Let me explain. I saw you and Justin speaking alone together at Lord and Lady Toller's ball. It appeared to me that you were gazing into each other's eyes with great affection. At that moment, I told myself that you were in love with him. I resolved to set you free that very evening so you could be with him."

She was quiet for a moment. When she spoke again, she sounded winded and breathless. "And you found that your assumption was incorrect this evening?"

"Yes." He held his arms still at his sides and squeezed his hands together in a supreme effort not to reach out and gather her close onto his chest. He wanted so badly to comfort her and at the same time ask her forgiveness for his foolish behavior. "When I saw you two together tonight, I believed you had decided to marry him. I confronted Justin in the library. I wanted to know if I was to wish him happy."

"He asked me to play along with him to provoke you. I believe he was hoping to make you jealous." She blushed rosily when she looked at him.

"I've been sorry I set you free since the night of the ball, but I was also thankful of the happiness I thought I had given to you. Justin explained that he had been offering to assist you while I was gone and anything that I saw that evening was simply affection between old friends."

"I'll only be truly happy if I'm with you, Robert."

"Come here. Let me hug you." He opened his arms wide and she ran into them. He wrapped his arms around her and he spoke into the silken strands of her hair. "I'm so sorry for all the pain and heartache I have caused you. I love you so much."

"I love you too."

He reluctantly stepped away from her and got down on one knee still clasping one of her hands in his own.

"You give me hope when I hear you say those words, Selina. Will you marry me and allow me to spend the rest of my life showing you how precious and dear you are to me?"

Selina smiled down at him through tears. "I would gladly, joyously consent to be your wife, Robert."

"I wish you both very happy." Miss Worth sniffled and wiped her nose with a handkerchief. "But, my lady, you should finish your meal. Lord Crestor needs to leave now."

Robert hastily stood up. "Did I bring you enough to eat, my love?"

Selina moved closer to his side until her lips were tantalizingly close to his own. "It's never enough, Robert. And I'm not speaking of food."

Ignoring the jarring sound of Miss Worth clearing her throat behind them, Robert and Selina treated themselves to a thrilling, passionate kiss. Only a taste of the romance and love to come when they lived their lives together as man and wife.

I Wish
for Your Kiss

by

Cynthia Moore

Christmas Lites

Dedication

Because this is a second chance story,
I would like to dedicate this book
to my doctors at Scripps
who saved my life and gave me a second chance:
Dr. Paul Hyde
Dr. Pushpendu Banerjee

Chapter One

December 1814

Justin Wexley, Marquess of Rockton, strode down the garden path, his gloved hands pushed deep inside the pockets of his coat. The underside of his boots ground against the hardened, icy surface of the gravel walkway. Although it was not as cold as the record-setting winter the year before, Justin was aware it had been several weeks since he had been outdoors without being covered from head to foot to guard against the prevailing frigid temperatures. Perhaps the inclement weather was a foreshadowing of heavy snowfall in time for Christmas, now only four days away.

It was good to slip out of the house for a brief period, no matter how chilly the temperature. He was troubled by a sense of confusion or perhaps it was unease. Whatever the problem, it made him feel unbalanced; he certainly was not his usual confident, assured self. For his own peace of mind, he needed to determine the cause of his discomfort as quickly as possible.

He had made a last minute decision to spend the holiday with his friend from Eton College days, Edward Teague, the Earl of Norton, and his family on their estate not far from Dover. Edward had been married to his wife Mary for several years. They had a brood of three children, one only a few months old. Both Edward and Mary were doting parents, believing their love and affection for their offspring would best be shown by including them in their daily activities, not simply consigning the children to the nursery to be looked upon at very brief periods throughout the day.

The children didn't bother Justin. The infant was usually sleeping in its cot while the other two played quietly with their toys or listened with rapt attention as their parents read them stories. He had a hunch the cause of his preoccupation and restlessness was an unexpected visitor by the name of Miss Catherine Simms, the only daughter of the late Viscount Meyer.

Miss Simms had abruptly appeared on the scene three days ago. She was a childhood friend of Lady Norton. Edward had explained to him that the two had corresponded over the years, but the distractions of a growing family combined with the sudden passing of both Miss Simms's parents meant there had been little or no opportunity to meet each other in person. A chance encounter in London a month previously had resulted in Lady Norton issuing an invitation to her friend to join her and her family for the Christmas holiday.

Justin prided himself on his ability to avoid the Parson's mousetrap and the cunning wiles of unmarried ladies. He was content with the way he lived his life. He could see no need to saddle himself with a wife who had nothing of interest to say and would never love him. He had an heir; his cousin was a hale and hearty young man. He was also smart and diligent. Justin had absolutely no qualms about leaving his estate and title to him.

That was not to say he was one to eschew the

company of ladies. Rather to the contrary, he usually attended some select suppers, breakfasts, and balls in London during the Season. As a wealthy peer and owner of a profitable estate, Justin was well aware that the members of the elite society he was a part of would frown upon him if he never consented to make an appearance at such events.

He believed that he conducted himself with the utmost decorum and graciousness in these circumstances. He made a concerted effort to be amusing and well-informed, no matter how trying the situation, throughout all of his encounters with the ladies. Justin was aware that many thought him aloof; hard to please. Their opinions hadn't mattered to him, until now.

Justin took a deep breath and sighed. Frosty white mist swirled in front of his face. He tucked the wool scarf more securely underneath his chin as he stared directly ahead without actually seeing the landscape. Unusual sensations had taken over his very being; absentmindedness, loss of appetite, the inability to sleep, tossing and turning in his bed at night. He wasn't ill, but he certainly didn't feel like himself. Surely, there was a simple explanation for the state he was in, but a sinking sensation in the pit of his stomach was a precipitate indication that he knew perfectly well what ailed him. He noticed a wooden bench near the path, underneath a small grove of leafless aspen trees and walked closer. He lifted one booted foot to the edge of the seat and contemplated the dappled white trunks on the trees in front of him.

Miss Simms had arrived suddenly, without warning. He remembered comparing her hasty entrance to a whirlwind; she seemed to appear and overshadow the space with her presence in a matter of moments. After the butler Grayson announced her, nothing was destined to be as it had been ever again. She entered the room on the butler's heels, hastily pulling on the strings of her fur-lined hat, brushing away Grayson's efforts to assist her. She tossed the hat, along with her gloves, onto the seat of an empty chair and rushed headlong into the open arms of her friend. From there, she made a quick turn to acknowledge her host and without pause, swiftly moved across the room to peek at the sleeping infant.

The other two children, who only moments before had been playing with their toys in the corner of the room, stood in unison, loudly questioning the newcomer if she had brought them any books.

Miss Simms laughed merrily with a cheery, tinkling sound. "Hello, Lady Beatrice and Lord Peter Moss, I can't tell you that. You must wait for Christmas."

Mary put her hand on her friend's arm. "Catherine, you must meet our other guest, Justin Wexley, the Marquess of Rockton. He and Edward attended college together. My good friend, Miss Simms."

Miss Simms turned to him, and he saw her face clearly for the first time. Her auburn colored hair was in some disarray after the hurried removal of her hat; wisps of the curly, silken strands had fallen from their fastenings to frame her heart-shaped face. She had a dainty nose, tipped slightly upward at the end. Her clear, creamy complexion was illuminated by a pair of large brown eyes, surrounded by thick, dark lashes. Her eyes appeared to twinkle as she smiled engagingly at him with full, ruby red lips. "My lord; it is a pleasure to meet one of Edward's schoolmates."

He took her proffered hand in his own and bowed over it. "It has been many years since Edward and I have walked those lofty corridors, but we have managed to stay close. I'm honored as well to meet a special friend of Mary's. Please call me Justin. We are to be a part of the family for the holidays, after all."

"Very well; I'm Catherine."

He released her hand and studied her lovely face as she stared up at him. "How did you and Mary first become acquainted?"

"Our families owned adjoining houses in Mayfair, and our nannies were sisters. I was an only child and Mary had two brothers. It was inevitable that we would become inseparable."

"I can picture the scene now. Your two nannies enjoying a good gossip on a park bench while you both sneak away and hide behind a nearby tree or bush. I feel sorry for the poor ladies' nerves."

Her brown eyes widened when she heard his observation. "However did you guess?"

He grinned at her. "Something in your manner when you stormed into the room, similar to a fresh breeze blowing off the ocean. It made me think you were probably a busy, lively imp as a child. I imagine you were the one that coerced Mary into misbehaving?"

She smiled at him and once again filled the room with her joyful, merry laughter. "I can think of a few instances when it was her idea but yes, the decision to make mischief was usually done at my instigation."

A portly lady appeared at the door shrouded in a heavy shawl. "Miss Simms, come to your room to change before you catch your death of cold."

"I will be there shortly."

Justin cocked one eyebrow. "Who is that worthy woman?"

Catherine's unblemished cheeks turned rosy. "My companion, Miss Wicker, she is forever worrying about cold drafts in large houses such as this."

"Come join me in the nursery when you have finished."

Justin registered a moment of surprise when he heard Mary's voice behind him. He had been so caught up in his discussion with Catherine he had forgotten there were others in the room. A sense of regret panged him as she turned away to follow her companion.

Justin lowered his foot to the ground and slapped his gloved hands against his thighs. It was time to saddle his horse and go for a quick ride. It was just the thing to clear his mind of its muddled, nonsensical ideas.

****

A couple of hours later, Justin handed over his well-exercised horse to Edward's head groom. "Rub Atlas down well, Turner. I put him through his paces today."

"Yes, my lord. I'll see to it that he receives the best of care."

Justin studied the bright, candlelit reflections on the windows as he walked from the stables to the front of the house. Darkness came quickly this time of year and the warm glow was a welcoming sight on what promised to be a very cold night. Before he could stop himself, his thoughts went back to Miss Simms—Catherine. So much for his good intentions! He gave himself up to the inevitable and acknowledged the ideas that were going through his mind. Would she and Mary be closeted away in the nursery once again as they had been quite often since her arrival, playing with the children? He imagined they chattered and gossiped about their acquaintances, offered opinions on garments, and gave each other a basic critique of the activities in their daily lives. Or was it possible Catherine had already dressed for dinner and was, at this moment, cooling her heels alone in the drawing room waiting for someone to join her?

Justin vaulted up the outside steps as he imagined such a possibility and thrust his gloves into Grayson's waiting hands. The quicker he changed, the sooner he could join her. If he could engage Catherine for a few minutes in a somber discussion on the merits of some banal topic of mutual interest, he was certain he would arrive at the same conclusion as he had with all previous marriageable women. With their heads full of the rules of etiquette and the pressing need to make a good impression on an eligible peer of the realm, the ladies were either unable or unwilling to lend their thoughts to other serious and thought-provoking matters to liven up a dialogue. He would lose this silly attraction for Miss Simms within moments once she proved herself to be as dull as all the others.

He pushed open the door to his bedchamber. "Higgins!"

"Yes, my lord?" His valet walked out of the dressing room holding a pressed and starched cravat in his hand.

"I'm going downstairs a bit early this evening. I need you to perform your magic and turn me out in double-time."

Higgins draped the cravat over a nearby chair before turning to make his way to the clothes press. "The black coat and pantaloons with the royal blue waistcoat, my lord?"

Justin shrugged himself out of his coat and untied his crumpled cravat. "That will be fine, Higgins."

A short time later, Justin strode down the main staircase brushing absentmindedly at an imagined speck of dust on his coat sleeve. He walked soft-footed down the hallway to the drawing room door, intending to reach it before Grayson became aware of his presence. It wouldn't do for the butler to announce him. If Catherine was indeed inside the room on her own, Justin wished to catch her by surprise. It would give him a better chance to observe what activity, if any, she was preoccupied with at the moment.

He turned the knob on the door and pushed it open. He was gratified to see Catherine sitting unaccompanied on the sofa. She had an open book on her lap and a wooden basket stuffed with what appeared to be an assortment of colored thread balanced on a cushion beside her.

"My lo...Justin! Are you looking for Edward? I don't believe he is down yet." She smiled at him and started to rise from her seat.

"No, please. Stay where you are. I am content to wait for the others in your company, if you have no objection." He raised his brows and grinned at her.

"Of course, come join me." She pointed at the basket. "Miss Wicker will be returning momentarily. She was sorting her embroidery thread and suddenly realized a favorite color was missing. She has gone to search her bags vowing to retrieve the treasured article."

Justin heard her words with a sense of panic. There wasn't much time for him to judge Catherine's worthiness. He must forge ahead and complete as much of his observation as quickly as possible. "You are reading a novel? Are you a fan of the Gothic romances that I understand are currently the rage?"

Catherine's jubilant laughter filled the room. "Heavens, no! I must confess I am drawn to less fanciful subjects in the novels I read. At present I'm perusing Lord Bryon's latest poem *The Corsair.* Have you heard of it?"

"How could I not be aware of it? Did it not sell over ten thousand copies on the first day of release?"

"Yes, and twenty-five thousand in the first month." She looked down at the book in her lap and frowned. "I wish I could experience the same enthusiasm for the piece as those who rushed to purchase it obviously felt."

"You do not like it?"

He heard her sigh before looking up and smiling at him. "I have never been a fan of Byron's poetry. I promised an acquaintance of mine, who was one of those initial ten thousand admirers, to read the work after she had prattled on and on about it whenever we met each other in town."

"I don't believe I have ever heard anyone complain about the man's writing. What is the source of your grievance with him? Can you identify it?" Justin held his breath for a moment after he spoke. He didn't believe she had actually read a page of the piece. He was ready to wager she would make up an absurd excuse for her feelings of dislike. She must do anything to avoid actually making intelligent observations; another silly, vapid female to be sure.

She stared into the fire for a moment before turning to face him. "I've never met him, but I have heard tales of his vainness and conceit. Such traits are obviously

177

hard to admire in a person. They are even harder to applaud in a long work of poetry such as this. When I read about the hero in the tale, Conrad, I have a good sense that I'm experiencing the character of Lord Bryon as well."

Her answer surprised him. Could it be that she thought about subjects other than marriage and the weather? Perhaps she was just good at prevaricating. He must delve deeper. "Give me some examples."

"Conrad is continually claiming to be chivalrous and brave. Yet when the time comes to prove his assertions he is too weak. Others must defend him and his honor." She sighed again. "I suppose those who enjoy this work would argue that the interest in the story comes from Conrad's ability to rally those around him to come to his aid, but I find no delight in it."

"I finally found the thread at the bottom of my trunk." Miss Wicker stood in the doorway triumphantly brandishing a bit of red string from underneath a pile of several woolen shawls draped across her broad shoulders. She turned to pull the topmost cover more closely across her shoulders and started. "My lord, I didn't see you! Forgive me."

Justin came to his feet, preparing to leave. He had much to think of. "It is of no matter, Miss Wicker. Your mistress and I were passing the time until the others join us for dinner."

He turned to find Catherine standing next to him. "I enjoyed our discussion, my lo…Justin. I would be interested in hearing your thoughts on the piece as well."

"I must admit I have not read it."

"Oh no! How thoughtless of me!" She placed her hand on his sleeve. "I hope my comments haven't ruined it for you."

"To the contrary, you have greatly piqued my interest."

Her hand dropped away from his arm. She sighed. "I'm very glad to hear that. Even though it is not to my taste, you might find the tale enjoyable."

"I intend to discover if that is so at my first opportunity. Excuse me; I must retrieve something from my room. I will see you both at dinner."

Chapter Two

"There, they should sleep for a couple of hours." Mary tucked the blanket around her sleeping son and smoothed back a lock of tousled hair from his forehead. She turned to do the same for her daughter and then motioned for Catherine to follow her. "You can keep me company while I feed the baby."

Silently, Catherine walked behind her friend into a cozy room off the nursery. A fire was burning merrily in the hearth. Two overstuffed Queen Anne chairs flanked the fireplace. Catherine waited for Mary to settle herself with the infant tucked at her breast, suckling noisily before she perched herself on the edge of the other chair.

"Are you feeling well, Catherine?"

Mary's sudden question startled her. She sat up straight against the cushions and faced her friend. "Yes, of course. Why do you ask?"

"There have been a few times I've said something to you and you haven't answered me. It happened last night after dinner as well as this morning. You appear to be miles away."

"I…I hadn't realized. I'm sorry."

"Are you worried about something? Have you heard from Lord Greer?"

"Yes. The plans have been made and a date is set…I don't wish to speak of it, Mary."

"Very well. I simply wanted to offer the assurance

that Edward and I would attend if you feel you need our support."

"Thank you both very much for the kind offer. Lord Greer and I have agreed to attend to the matter with a minimum of fuss and fanfare." She paused and cleared her throat. "I wanted to ask you; what do you know of Lord Rockton?"

"Lord…Justin? What do you wish to know?"

"I have heard rumors of his aversion to marriage. I was wondering if the stories were true."

Mary didn't seem surprised by her query. "Of course, I haven't known him nearly as long as Edward has. I met him just before our marriage. I do remember wondering aloud one day at Justin's ongoing single state. Edward just shrugged his shoulders and told me he thought Justin preferred to show his interest in women in a slow, deliberate, less obvious manner. I'm not certain if Edward was entirely serious, but he also said he believed by the time Justin decides he has found his special lady, she will already be betrothed or married to someone else."

"Do you think Lord Rockton isn't against marriage? He is simply taking his time finding the right woman to be part of his life?"

"As unusual as this might sound for a peer in his position, I'm not sure if he is truly searching for a wife. We have met him at several social functions in London, but I got the impression he was merely making requisite appearances. I noticed he would leave the gathering as soon as it was polite to do so. He never made an attempt to single out a woman or even to have a lengthy discussion with a lady in my recollection."

Catherine frowned as she tried to make sense of

what Mary had told her. "Perhaps he doesn't want to be saddled with a wife. From your observations, it sounds as if he is avoiding female company altogether."

"I wouldn't go so far as to say that, my dear. I am reminded of one evening when Justin admitted to Edward in my presence that he had narrowly avoided participating in a duel after another man accused him of making untoward advances to his betrothed. However, when Edward cautioned him and spoke of his duties to his family name and properties, Justin boasted that he would have absolutely no qualms handing over the running of his estate to his heir if anything should happen to him."

"Could it be that he prefers to dally with women who are already married or spoken for? It sounds as if he does have an aversion to marriage."

Mary moved the baby to her other side and adjusted the tiny head in the crook of her arm. "No! I could never think that Justin would deliberately trifle with a lady. Perhaps he had a bad experience with someone who broke his heart. I do wish a special woman who could love and care for him would come into his life. I'm certain that he must capture the ladies' interests at any public event he attends. You must admit he is a very handsome man."

Catherine pictured Justin's long golden-hued hair that he wore tied back with a thin leather strap to fall in a silken mass across his broad shoulders. Fine, sandy colored brows, pronounced cheekbones and large green eyes. A classic, aristocratic nose that was slightly bent at the bridge hovered over firm lips and a strong chin. A sense of contained strength radiated from him as well; a confirmation in Catherine's mind that he didn't shy away from challenging, physical activity. "I agree. I'm sure he receives a great deal of attention from women wherever he goes."

"Then there shouldn't be a lack of opportunity for him to eventually meet the right woman to love."

****

Justin paced across the brick floor of the orangery. The heat from the furnace tucked inside the north-facing stone wall of the building kept the interior of the room comfortably warm even on this cold winter day. Filtered sunlight peeped through the clouds; radiating across the large windows lining the south side of the structure illuminating the bright green, yellow and orange fruits hanging on several lime, lemon and orange trees inside the space.

Justin paid no attention to his surroundings. He was in a quandary. His opportune discussion with Catherine yesterday had not gone as planned. He had never encountered a woman like her. Her intelligent, thoughtful replies to his questions left him perplexed and bewildered. So much so that last evening at dinner he had barely been able to converse; only offering short, terse replies whenever he was addressed. Edward had noticed his preoccupation and asked if he was feeling quite the thing after the ladies had left the table. He had managed to assure his friend that he was fine by coming up with a story about his crops and his concern over their low output the previous summer.

Now he frowned down at the bricks covering the floor of the hothouse and spoke his frustration aloud. "Damn! What have I started?"

"Sorry? Oh, excuse me, Lor…Justin. I didn't mean to disturb you."

He spun around at the sound of Catherine's voice to discover the object of his chagrin standing near the sitting area close to the heated wall. She was warmly bundled in a cherry-red, fur-lined pelisse with shiny, black leather boots covering her feet. She turned and walked away from him heading toward the doorway. He called out to her. "Wait. Don't go."

She stopped and faced him. "I don't wish to intrude."

"You're not intruding. It would be a pleasure to have your company. Please sit down."

She retraced her steps, lowered herself onto the edge of a cushioned chair and clasped her hands in her lap. "Mary...Mary will join us in a minute. She is making sure the children are settled. This...This is a lovely room."

Her hesitant speech after hearing his untimely outburst caused Justin to realize Catherine probably sensed his frustration. He must soothe her ruffled composure and make an attempt to set her at her ease. However, with Mary's impending arrival, he needed to quickly strike up a conversation with her. He sat on the overstuffed sofa across from Catherine and forced himself to speak in a casual manner. "It is wonderful to enjoy a bit of the outdoors inside a warm room on a chilly winter day such as this."

"I couldn't agree more. Do...Do you have an orangery on your estate?" She spoke softly, keeping her gaze lowered and fixed upon her hands.

"Yes, I do. It is quite similar in shape and size to this one." He answered her, making certain his voice sounded composed and relaxed.

She raised her head to look directly at him. "Where

is your estate located? Is it large?"

"Not far from London; just outside of Newbury. I own about fifty acres of land. Tell me, have you always lived in London?" He was relieved to see she appeared to be disregarding his earlier regrettable outburst. She kept her gaze aimed at his face.

"When my parents were alive we had a small estate in Bath. That was our principle residence. My mother and I would travel to London and stay there with my father when Parliament was in session. On occasion, we would also rent lodgings in Brighton and reside there for a few weeks during the summer months." She settled herself back against the cushions on the chair.

"Do you prefer Bath to Brighton or vice versa?" He pressed on with his queries, eager to hear her replies.

"As you know, Bath is a refined, genteel town known for its restorative waters. Brighton in the summer time is a happy, carefree place to enjoy the ocean breezes and the seashore. They are each special places in very different ways," she finished in a vague manner.

Was she trying to avoid giving him a detailed answer to his question? He must press her for more. "If you had to live in one city only, which would you choose? Give me your reasons."

She stared at the ground, frowning. "If I was forced to pick one...I suppose it must be Bath. A seaside town such as Brighton is fine for a short visit when the weather is nice, but the city lacks other essential things that I deem important for daily living."

"What would those things be?"

She smiled at him and Justin was momentarily dazzled. He made himself concentrate on what she was saying. "As you probably have deduced, I enjoy reading."

"Bath has several circulating libraries and reading rooms to choose from. My mother and I made a point to visit one every week when we were in town. We also enjoyed going to the Upper Assembly Rooms. Brighton doesn't have a building as elegant and so specially intended for dancing and musical entertainment."

"What of the Prince George's penchant for Brighton? I take it you don't share in his enthusiasm for the city?"

Her cheeks flushed pink. "He simply found it convenient to take his paramour there. He hid her away in a cottage."

"Whose paramour?" Mary strode into the room and sat down next to Justin on the sofa.

Catherine's tinkling laugh rang out in the room before she answered. "We were discussing Prince George and his fondness for Brighton. I believe he goes to the city simply because he can hide there with Mrs. Fitzherbert."

Mary giggled as well. "I don't believe the prince can avoid public notice for long wherever he might go."

"I don't think he will escape notoriety in this instance either. It is rumored he has begun discussions with Mr. John Nash to create a grand pavilion in Brighton."

Catherine leaned forward in her chair and gasped. "After what happened when the prince hired Henry Holland to design and build Carlton House? You can't believe our government will countenance another exorbitant project such as that?"

Justin managed to hide his surprise when Catherine was able to identify another architect with one of his projects; no matter how famous they both were. There were no young ladies in his acquaintance who could speak with any knowledge at all on building styles or their designers. "I'm betting Prinny will have his way."

Mary sighed. "I'm not one to condone speaking harshly about our monarch but I fear the King was overly harsh with him as a boy. Now that the prince is older, it seems he will stop at nothing to get what he wants."

"Nor does he concern himself with how much something costs."

Edward strolled into the room. "Of whom do you speak, Catherine?"

Mary turned and held her hand out to her husband across the back of the sofa. "We were lamenting the excessive spending habits of Prince George, my dear."

Edward picked up his wife's hand and kissed it. "Too much rein as a child. Now that he is allowed to roam free, no one can catch him."

"Just as I said before you joined us." Mary smiled at him. "Come sit down."

Edward chuckled. "Perhaps later, my love; I came to challenge Justin to a game of billiards."

Justin stood up; acknowledging the brief opportunity to speak with Catherine alone was over. He bowed to both of the ladies. "I enjoyed conversing with you both."

"Justin, I wanted to remind you," Mary called out as he turned away to follow Edward. "Tomorrow is Christmas Eve. We are going to take the carriage out to collect greenery to decorate the house after breakfast. Do you wish to join us?"

"Please come." Catherine grinned at him. "We need

an extra pair of strong arms."

"We intend to bring the children as well. We can't stay out in the cold too long, and there won't be much room in the carriage." Edward spoke from the doorway. "Why don't you and Catherine take the horse cart, Justin? The old mare Betty is reliable, and the cart is sturdy. You two should be able to gather enough greenery to decorate the entire dining room at the very least."

Justin struggled to remain composed as he was handed a rare opportunity to spend some time alone with Catherine. "Of course I will help. I wouldn't miss such a chance."

"Wonderful." Catherine clapped her hands together and laughed. "However, I must warn you that I probably won't be able to offer you much assistance other than to point out the most favorable bushes and plants to collect cuttings. Miss Wicker is certain to insist I bundle up against the cold from the top of my head to the bottom of my toes."

Justin grinned back at her, he could think of no circumstance that could ruin such an opportune occasion for him. "Don't concern yourself. I will rely on you to spot the choicest shrubbery. We will assemble a grand pile of greenery for the dining room together."

Chapter Three

They all met in the dining room a few hours later. Catherine noted with appreciation the large, sparkling chandelier centered over gleaming white plates framed by highly-polished silverware and glassware as she took her seat at the table. When everyone had made their way to their own chairs, Grayson poured red wine into each of their glasses while two other servants brought in the first course.

"I hope you enjoy the parsnip soup." Mary picked up the serviette next to her plate and put it on her lap. "It is one of my favorites. Cook mixes in some of the juices from the roasted beef to give the broth a special flavor. I ask her to make it every year at this time."

Catherine picked up her spoon and took a sip from her bowl. "It's delicious. I never thought of mixing meat juices in a vegetable soup. The taste is very unique."

"We are lucky to have such prolific crops even in winter. My wife never lacks for a variety of vegetables to bring to our table." Edward took a sip of his wine. "What of your land, Justin? I'm sorry to hear your crop production has suffered."

Catherine looked up from her soup. "Is there a problem? Perhaps I could help."

Justin stared at her from his seat on the other side of the table. "What do you know of farming?"

Catherine could feel her checks flushing. Perhaps

she had spoken out of turn. She lowered her spoon to the tablecloth next to her bowl, clearing her throat before speaking. "I...I mentioned to you that I was an only child. I also told you my family had a small estate near Bath."

Justin didn't flinch. "Yes you did. What do those things have to do with giving me farming advice?"

Catherine had a sense he believed she was wasting his time. It was common to think that a woman should never show an interest in something that was clearly a gentleman's concern. She spoke up quickly, anxious to prove she knew what she was talking about. "Even though we owned a small estate with a modest amount of open land for crops, my father was continually looking for ways to increase our harvest outputs. He discovered a few books that offered sound ideas. I spent many evenings with him in his library discussing possible planting alternatives."

Justin lowered his brows. She could see tiny wrinkles crisscrossing his forehead. "Your father had no help? No estate manager to speak to?"

"He had a man who was there when he inherited the estate, a Mr. Bender. He was hired as a boy by my grandfather to work in the gardens. When my father began his research, Mr. Bender was elderly and set in his ways. He wasn't interested in trying new things and refused to talk about alternatives. I believe I served as an attentive audience. Our discussions eventually helped my father to clarify and choose the proper scheme that doubled the output of our crops in two years' time."

"That is certainly remarkable. I, for one, would be very interested to hear what your father decided to do." Edward raised his wine glass toward Justin. "Come now, old man, it can't hurt to listen, and you might discover what has caused your problems as well."

"I am eager to hear what Catherine has to say." Justin turned away from her to address his friend. "I simply find it hard to believe that her father discovered a magic remedy to increase crop production that presumably very few people know about or are privy to."

The door to the dining room opened. Servants brought in plates containing slices of roasted beef, boiled potatoes, and carrots. Catherine waited to speak again until everyone had been served.

"As a matter of fact, the method we choose is far from a closely-guarded secret. It was started by a man who had a farm in Hungerford, Berkshire. I believe that isn't very far from your estate in Newbury. He passed away in seventeen forty-one. Have you heard of Mr. Tull and his writings?"

Justin was cutting a piece of his beef when she spoke. His knife slipped from his fingers and clattered onto the edge of his plate. "Is he the one who invented the seed drill?"

"Yes, the very man!" Catherine answered, delighted he knew something of what she was speaking of.

"I was told the cost of the drill was exorbitant," Justin replied in a dismissive manner.

She wasn't about to allow him to cast off the subject of their discussion in such a way. "It was expensive, but when my father used the hoeing methods described in Tull's book along with his seed drill, we were able to double the crop yield. It was well worth the extra money."

"What is the title of this book?" Mary took a roll

from a basket that was placed in front of her by one of the servants."

"It is quite long; *The New Horse-houghing Husbandry: or An Essay on the Principles of Tillage and Vegetation.*" Catherine took a deep breath and speared a piece of carrot with her fork. Hopefully, just the fact that she could recite such a title from memory would be proof enough to Justin that she was very familiar with the book and its contents.

"I will ask my estate manager to obtain a copy as soon as possible." Edward made a signal to Grayson. He stepped forward from his post in the corner and refilled everyone's glasses.

"What do you believe actually made the difference in your father's crop yields?"

Catherine thought over Justin's question for a moment before answering. "The book explained that frequent hoeing of the soil allows important gases and moisture in the atmosphere to more easily penetrate down to the roots of the crop. Once the soil was properly conditioned using the horse-drawn hoe method, and the seeds were dropped at equal distances at a correct depth into the ground using the seed drill, better crop output was almost certain to occur."

"Assuming you had adequate rain storms throughout the year as well?" Justin pushed his plate away. One of the servants came to the table to collect it.

"Of course, my father made a point to gather as much rain water as possible to use to irrigate the crops when storms were infrequent. We also had a fairly large stream that ran through our property."

Justin took a drink of wine. "I will discuss what you have suggested with my estate manager when I return."

"I'm glad. I sincerely hope the knowledge I gained from my father's research will help you." Catherine turned to Mary who had stayed quiet through most of their discussion. "I'm sorry, dear. I didn't intend to monopolize the conversation. Will Peter and Beatrice be joining us for Christmas Eve dinner tomorrow night?"

"Oh yes, they wouldn't miss their chance to pretend to be all grown up. It only happens a few times a year." Mary looked pensive for a moment and then smiled at her. "You know, when we were little, I remember feeling sorry for you because you were an only child. But now that I hear of your talks with your father about his crops and I think of the many times I joined you and your mother for tea to listen to you both debate about your favorite books and poetry, I realize how close you were to both of them. I'm certain it didn't matter to you that you were on your own."

Catherine took a deep breath, staring blankly at the tablecloth. How much she missed her father and mother! She roused herself to answer, "You're right, Mary. I was never lonely while my parents were alive."

****

Justin strode down the front steps and walked toward the groom who was standing in the drive next to a rustic, wooden cart.

"Tell me the name of this worthy beast?" he asked as the groom handed him the reins attached to the head of an elderly horse at the front of the equipage.

"She be called Betty, my lord. The stable master says she's a sure bet. Maybe not so fast any longer but fixed and steady. She'll get you where you be wantin' to go and back."

Justin studied the mare. The animal made no

movement to acknowledge him. She faced forward, staring toward the stable area. Justin imagined the horse was already pinning away for a carrot and her bed of warm hay. "That is very comforting to hear."

"What's wrong, Justin? Betty's a great old beast. She might be slow, but she's reliable."

Justin turned around to see Edward and Mary coming toward him. Edward had Peter and Beatrice's hands clasped in his own. Mary clutched the baby in her arms. All were dressed warmly. "Your groom has just informed me of those facts, Edward."

"She's quite gentle, Justin. Peter and Beatrice have both taken turns at the reins with no mishap." Mary smiled reassuringly at him.

A clatter of hooves could be heard over their voices, and the family's crested traveling carriage came around the corner of the house to come to a stop near the cart.

"Miss Simms, promise me you'll keep yourself covered!"

Justin turned at the sound of Miss Wicker's agitated voice.

"I promise! Don't worry so. I'll be fine." Catherine's slightly muffled, tinkling laugh rang out as walked down the stairs and joined them. "I'm so sorry for coming late. As you can see, Miss Wicker did insist I bundle up."

Justin studied her attire. She wore the same red, fur-lined pelisse from the day before. Additionally, a matching red cap was pulled down over her ears, quite effectively covering most of her hair; a thick, woolen scarf was wrapped around her neck, pulled up over her chin, mouth, and nose. Her gloved hands were thrust inside a furry muff. Only her eyes were visible, twinkling merrily from out of the edge of the coverings. "I can't imagine you'll feel anything other than warmth dressed as you are."

"I did warn you. But there is no reason for concern. My costume won't hamper my greenery-spotting abilities in the least."

With her scarf covering most of her face, Justin couldn't see Catherine's expression, but he imagined she was smiling at him. He intended to fully enjoy the time he had been given to spend alone with his companion. "I'll have to keep a watch on that hat. You won't be much help to me if it should fall down over your eyes."

She reached up to push the hat back off of her forehead. "Don't worry. As soon as we are out of sight of the house, I'm going to take it off."

"Are you certain? Your ears will get cold, and I'll have to face Miss Wicker's wrath." Justin shivered inwardly as he imagined what would happen if he was to somehow displease her formidable companion.

"I'll answer to her if she should find out. I have had to deal with her displeasure many times in the past," Catherine replied nonchalantly.

"Do you purposely ignore her wishes?" Justin helped Catherine step into the cart.

She settled herself on the thick blanket the groom had thoughtfully placed across the wooden seat. "No, not at all. It's very hard to disregard Miss Wicker's whims, especially as they almost always pertain to her opinions on the best methods to keep warm. Obviously, we live in a place where it is rarely hot, even in the summer. I simply don the extra shawls, caps, and gloves under her watchful eyes and then remove most of the bits and pieces when she is no longer in the vicinity."

Justin walked around to the other side of the cart and climbed in. The groom handed him the reins.

"My lord, take these for your hands." Grayson appeared at his elbow holding out a pair of worn gloves.

"You don't want to ruin yours on the prickly holly bushes." Edward called as he climbed into the carriage. "I had my man get you an old pair from the stables. There is also some gardening scissors inside the front compartment to cut the thicker branches with."

"Follow us," Mary added from her seat as she handed the baby to her husband. "We'll stop at a spot where it's easier for the children to reach the greenery. The place where you two should collect is just beyond."

"I understand." Justin took the old gloves from Grayson and looked for a place to put them. There wasn't much extra room inside the tiny vehicle. He was aware of a soothing, warm sensation inside his chest he guessed was caused by the heat radiating from Catherine's body just inches from his side.

"I'll take them."

Catherine reached across, and their gloved fingers tangled together for a brief second. Justin heard her muffled gasp as she swiftly moved her hand away and dropped the gloves in her lap.

"We're off." A sudden thrill of pleasure went through him as he noticed Catherine's reaction. Could it be she was affected by their close proximity as well? It should prove to make their outing a very interesting one if that was the case. He flicked the reins and urged the horse forward to follow behind the carriage.

As soon as they rounded a corner and moved away from the house, Catherine yanked the hat off of her head and pulled the scarf down from her nose and mouth.

"There. That is so much more comfortable."

Out of the corner of his eye, Justin saw her straighten her glossy curls with a gloved hand. He had a sudden image of his own fingers stroking the silky strands. His heart pounded erratically, and he took a deep breath in an effort to calm himself. "Promise… promise me that you will cover up again if you get cold."

"Of course, I promise. But I'm certain there will be no need." Her joyous laugh rang out. "Oh, it's so nice to be outdoors in the fresh air. Look, there is not a cloud in the sky!"

As he urged the mare forward, Justin realized that anyone would be hard-pressed to stay gloomy in her company for long. Not only was she obviously a happy person, she was intelligent and a lively conversationalist. It was a joy to be around her.

"We'll pull over here." Edward called out as the carriage moved to the side of the track and stopped. "The better spot for you is just around the corner."

"We'll do our best to fill up the cart," Justin replied as they drew up alongside.

"See that you do!" Mary emerged from the carriage and with the help of a groom, guided Peter and Beatrice down the steps. "I want my dining table to glow with an abundance of Christmas cheer this evening."

Catherine waved at them as their horse ambled by. "Such dear children. They have very happy lives. Edward and Mary are obviously devoted parents."

"Your mother and father sound as if they were loving, caring people as well. They certainly included you in most aspects of their lives."

"Yes, they…they were quite wonderful." She

became silent, staring down at her hands.

Justin guided the mare around a bend in the road and maneuvered the cart to the edge of the road. He dropped the reins in his lap and turned to face Catherine, putting his hand on her arm. "I'm sorry. I didn't mean to make you sad. I shouldn't have mentioned them."

She raised her head and looked at him; a few tears glistened in her brown eyes. They fell, cascading in tiny, liquid rows down her cheeks. "There is no need for you to apologize. I adored them. I always have happy memories when I discuss my parents. But sometimes, when I think of them, I feel a deep, throbbing pain in my chest and it makes me cry. I miss them so much."

"Do you want to talk about them now?"

She smiled at him with trembling lips as she reached up to wipe the moisture from her face with one gloved hand. "I'm sure you're wondering... "

"You don't have to tell me."

"I want to. It...it was a carriage accident. They had gone to visit friends on the other side of Bath. A fierce storm came out of nowhere as they headed home; dark, pitch-black sky, screaming wind, thunder and lightning. I was watching for them at the window hoping they hadn't ventured out. Their horses bolted, the carriage veered off the road and tipped over. They...they were thrown out...it was over in minutes."

Justin rubbed Catherine's arm. He could feel her pain. In the short time he had known her, it was obvious how close she had been to her parents. It was hard for him to imagine recovering from such a sudden, painful loss. "I'm so sorry."

She didn't say anything for several moments. "Thank...thank you. I'm glad you know what happened.

But enough of this now. It's Christmas Eve, and we have a job to do." She turned in her seat and gave him a lopsided grin.

He studied her face as he slowly removed his hand from her arm. "If you're certain you feel up to it?"

"Oh yes. I have been looking forward to this outing since Mary mentioned it to me yesterday morning. There!" She pointed at the trees bordering the meadow. "I see a prime specimen. It's very green and full of red berries. You will have no trouble reaching the branches. Where are the scissors?"

"They should be in the front compartment."

Catherine pulled the latch open and reached for the tool. She handed it to him. "Here. Cut as much as you can."

Justin gave her the reins before jumping out. He snipped all the greenery he could reach off of the holly bush and stacked the limbs in a pile before picking up the pieces and throwing them into the back of the cart. "That should cover most of the table."

"There is another shrub on the other side. Get a few specimens from there and then go to the pine tree to the left of that bush. We should have enough to decorate the entire dining room."

He cut several branches off of both plants, gathered the stacks, and loaded the greenery. Several pieces of holly dangled off to one side of the cart. He adjusted the pile, making certain all the branches were secure. "Should we look for any more?"

Catherine studied their collected treasure for a moment. "I can't imagine where we would put just one extra branch. It would certainly fall to the ground. Mary will be more than satisfied with what we have gathered."

"Our task was accomplished in record time. Do you want to take the cart a little further down the path or should we return to the house?"

"I need to get back. Miss Wicker will be frantic with worry. She probably imagines me with frostbite at this point."

Justin hoped she couldn't sense his disappointment. It was as if a dark cloud had suddenly covered up the sun. He slowly climbed into his seat and took the reins from her. He must do as she requested even though he wanted to have her to himself for as long as possible. "You exaggerate. The pile of coverings Miss Wicker had upon your person wouldn't allow any amount of chilly air to penetrate."

"I agree, but no matter how much she bundles me up, she is still apprehensive about the cold and the possibility of me becoming ill."

"Her concern for your well-being is admirable."

"She can be exasperating at times, but she means well."

Justin guided the horse into the front drive. He pulled back on the reins, waiting to speak until the horse had ambled to a stop. "I'm very glad she takes such good care of you."

Catherine looked at him with a bewildered expression on her face. "Why, thank you for saying something so nice, Justin."

A footman descended the front steps to help Catherine out of the cart. She gave the man her hand and stepped to the ground.

"I have no intention of merely being nice. I'm serious. The thought of you prostrate upon your bed with a fever brings grave thoughts to my mind and thunderous palpitations to my heart." He waved his gloved hand to her as she stood to one side staring at him. The old mare suddenly pulled the cart forward, making a run for the stables, obviously anticipating the food and shelter to be found there.

****

Justin took a deep breath of the cold air that surrounded him. He was back at his favored spot in the garden sitting on the bench. It was peaceful and quiet here. He could be alone with his confused and disordered thoughts. Today was Christmas. The days had rolled past in unhurried, relaxed succession. A majority of his free time had been spent in Catherine's company. They had discussed many interesting subjects and enjoyed numerous happy moments as well. He had initially been attracted by her beauty and vivaciousness. Now he was also impressed by the wealth of knowledge she possessed on many varied subjects as well as a practical and sensible outlook on life. Indeed, the deep understanding she had on the methods for increasing crop production would certainly help him to improve the output on his own estate. He was smitten. He should just admit the fact to himself and get on with the wooing process. But it was hard for him. After all the years of boasting that he was perfectly happy without a woman in his life, now it seemed he couldn't function properly without knowing this lady would be at his side for all time.

"Come, Peter. We won't walk too much farther. My arms will get tired holding your sister. It's good to get some fresh air."

Justin stood the moment he heard her sweet voice and laughter. She faced away from him and walked backward carrying Beatrice as she cajoled a reluctant Peter forward a few more steps. It was then that he noticed the patch of ice covering the pathway where an unsuspecting Miss Simms would place her booted foot in the next moment and most certainly slip and fall. He sprinted toward her, vaulting over the frozen strip on the ground.

"Allow me." He reached around, gathering her and the child close to his chest. "You didn't see the ice on the path. I was afraid you would harm yourself."

"Oh." She stopped mid-laugh, her breath coming out in short gasps. "Thank…thank you. That was very foolish of me."

He stared down at her full, red lips. They were trembling, perhaps because of shock and surprise at his sudden appearance. He couldn't help himself. He bent his head and kissed her.

She pulled away from him, clutching the child in her arms. "No!"

"No? What is wrong? I thought you enjoyed my company."

"I can't."

"You can't? Why?" He glared down at her as a sense of great frustration threatened to overwhelm him. "Are you promised to another? Betrothed?"

"As a matter of fact, I am."

He sucked in air through suddenly painful lungs. "I can't have misunderstood your interest in me."

She bounced Beatrice in her arms, never taking her gaze off of his face. "I thoroughly enjoyed our discussions, and of course I was attracted to you. You are a handsome, intelligent man. But your reputation precedes you. Lord Rockton, the peer who has sworn never to marry. Yes, I am promised to another. It's a long standing agreement between our deceased fathers. I never, ever imagined that you would form an attachment to me after all of your declarations against love and marriage."

"Miss Simms, I'm cold." Peter's teeth were chattering.

"I must go inside." She reached down to grasp the child's hand then turned and walked toward the house without looking back.

Chapter Four

Two years later

"We have been invited to spend the holidays at his cousin's home in Newbury. I have heard it is a very large estate and the house is beautiful. One day, John will inherit the title and the property. I'm very excited to see it." The pretty, young girl standing in the corner of the room smiled broadly.

"Who is this cousin?" Catherine, now the Dowager Viscountess Greer, felt a great sense of foreboding as she asked the question.

"Why, I thought you knew! John's cousin is Justin Wexley, Marquess of Rockton," answered her charge, Miss Elizabeth Croft.

"Lord Rockton?" She spoke his name aloud for the first time since she had said good-bye. The sudden pain in her chest was sharp and piercing.

"Are you acquainted with him?"

Catherine took a deep breath before speaking. "We have met, yes."

"I'm not surprised. Papa said you were bound to be quite familiar with most of the members of the *ton*. I'm so glad he hired you as my companion." Elizabeth came to a sudden stop with a look of wonder on her face. "I would never have met John if not for you, Lady Greer. You told me it was most proper to stroll in Hyde Park before midday, and he and his gentlemen friends happened to be there as well."

Catherine closed the book she had been reading and set it on a nearby table. "And you caught his interest and now you are betrothed. Thank you for your kind words, Elizabeth, but I'm certain the two of you would eventually have met even without my assistance. There is such a thing as fate, and I'm a firm believer in the concept. Why don't you go and change for dinner? I'll be up shortly."

Elizabeth walked across the room and put her hand on the door knob with a dreamy expression on her face. It was obvious the bulk of her thoughts were centered on her betrothed. "Very well, I think I'll wear the pale yellow gown tonight."

Catherine sighed as Elizabeth left the room. She stared at the glowing coals in the fireplace as she remembered Justin as she had last seen him on Christmas day almost two years ago. He had stood ramrod-straight, his expression grim, still managing to look heart-achingly handsome, glaring down at her in the entryway of Mary and Edward's home.

"I must return to Rockton. Many matters there require my urgent attention." He thrust his hat on his head and pulled his riding gloves over his hands.

Catherine knew a deep sense of regret as she realized his sudden haste to leave and return to his home was her fault. "I'm sorry you have to leave today. We have only just removed ourselves from the dinner table. You have no wish to eat a piece of mince pie or try the Christmas pudding?"

"I think you are well aware why I must not tarry here any longer. I wish you well, Miss Simms." He stared at her for a moment before bowing and turning to the door.

They were back to formality once again. "The same to you, Lord Rockton."

With tear-filled eyes, she had watched from a window as he climbed on his horse and rode away.

Three months later, she had married Colin Hopkins, Viscount Greer, in accordance with both of their fathers' wishes. Her residence in London was sold, and she and Miss Wicker settled into their new home on the outskirts of Guildford in Surrey. A few weeks after the ceremony, her new husband had announced his intention to join the cavalry in the effort to halt Napoleon's advancement across Europe. Not long after he left, she received a formal declaration that he had been killed in the Battle of Waterloo.

Catherine had been a widow for a year and a half. The time spent as a married woman had been so brief she sometimes found herself wondering if the event had actually taken place. Only the need to be consigned to the Dower House upon the arrival of the new heir and the daily reminder of the necessity to be attired in widow's weeds in the year following her husband's death made it a reality.

Her thoughts turned back to Lord Rockton. He had crossed her mind several times over the past two years. She couldn't help but wonder what it had been about her that made him ignore his vow to never become romantically involved with a woman of his class. As time passed, she reasoned she had placed too much importance on his kiss. It was simply a spur of the moment embrace caused by a fleeting attraction they both felt for each other. It meant nothing more than that.

Briefly, she contemplated refusing to accompany Elizabeth to the estate. But she soon realized that was something she would never do. She had been hired as a companion and would perform her duties until she was no longer needed. The notion of spending another lonely Christmas at the Dower House was quite depressing as well. Perhaps fate was playing a role in her life. She rose to her feet, shaking out her skirts. There was just enough time before dinner to dress and give orders to the maids to begin packing for a journey to Newbury.

****

"I'm very glad you and your family could join me for Christmas." Justin smiled warmly at his companion and then took a sip from his glass containing some of his estate's finest brandy.

"We were happy to come. You realize that you have invited a substantial amount of people to your home now that Selina and I are married?" The other gentleman rested his half-empty glass on the arm of his chair.

"Yes, of course. There is plenty of room for everyone. My cousin John, my Aunt Clara and John's betrothed Miss Elizabeth Croft will be here as well." Justin reminded himself to check with his butler to make certain his staff had everything they needed for the upcoming holiday celebration.

"Your heir John? He is getting married?" His companion sounded justifiably surprised.

"Yes. Imagine that? He met Miss Croft by chance in Hyde Park. He claims it was love at first sight." Justin was conscious of a sudden sense of regret as he imagined John's feelings of joy when he discovered his deep regard for the lady was reciprocated. Lucky man!

"What about you? I know I gave you a hard time

last year when I thought you and Selina had formed a lasting affection for each other. But I wish you would find a special woman, fall in love, and get married." The gentleman sounded wistful as he spoke the last sentence.

"There is no chance of that happening." Justin took another sip from his glass and stared at the glowing coals in the fireplace.

"No chance at all? Don't tell me you are continuing to avoid the company of eligible young ladies? I thought your declaration that you intended to wait for several years to get married was because you were preoccupied with your latest mistress or perhaps it was a way of keeping the overly ambitious mamas at bay." Lord Robert Crestor, Justin's best friend since childhood, paused for a moment, an expression of confusion on his face. "Perhaps my wife is correct. She believes your late mother is the cause of your hesitation to become attached to anyone."

"My mother? What has she to do with my lack of interest in getting married?" Justin put his glass down on the table and glared at Robert.

Robert stared back at him without flinching. "Everything, I should imagine. Don't you remember when we were boys, she was rarely at home. Always off to London with her 'friends'."

Justin came to his feet, unable to sit still any longer. He began pacing in front of the fireplace. "I was away at school most of the time. There was no reason for her to bide her time at the estate waiting for me to return home on leave."

Robert stood as well. "What about your father? I can remember walking into his study many times with you to find him sitting in his chair staring into the fire with a glass of brandy in his hand. When you would try to speak to him, he either wouldn't answer or would wave us out of the room."

Justin stopped pacing and leaned against the corner of the mantel. "My father had many things to take care of on the estate. They often caused him to worry. He didn't have the patience for rambunctious boys such as we were."

Robert faced him from the other side of the fireplace. "What about when we were older? I realize we never spoke of it, but you can't tell me that you weren't aware of the rumors about Lady Rockton?"

Justin sighed. "Yes, I know she had a reputation for having many lovers. My old nurse once admitted to me that my mother almost died when I was born. She vowed she would never be forced to have another child."

"That doesn't mean you never again spend time with your spouse." Robert pursed his lips and frowned. "I have spoken enough about Lady Rockton. You are forever boasting about how you manage to avoid the Parson's mousetrap. Has there never been a woman who caught your interest?"

"Uh, no...no never." Justin had spent many hours thinking about what exactly had transpired between Catherine and him during that Christmas celebration. He had come to the conclusion that he had behaved badly. Her superior intelligence and stimulating conversation had thrown him off balance, so to speak. He had misread her feelings because of the inspiration and pleasure he had experienced in her company. It had never crossed his mind that she could already have been spoken for.

"Come now, Justin we have been best friends

forever. I can sense some hesitation in your answer. There must have been someone."

"There was a lady once...I met her two years ago at a house party. You remember when I stayed with the Earl of Norton for the Christmas holidays?"

"Edward Teague, our schoolmate from Eton?"

"Yes, the very man. The lady in question was a particular friend of Edward's wife Mary. She was visiting them as well. When we were first introduced, I noted that she was quite a lovely and vivacious woman. I assumed she would be another simpering miss with her head full of nothing but the usual ability to comment on the state of the weather. I was determined to avoid her."

"Poor lady; were there others in the gathering that she could converse with?"

"There was only Edward, Mary, and their children; one who was an infant at the time. So, yes, with such a small party, it became quickly apparent to me that to refrain from speaking to her entirely would be very rude on my part."

Robert grinned at him. "I'm glad you came to your senses."

"Thank you. You know I'm not a bad sort over all."

"Oh, no, you're not a bad person. You're a good, kind, caring gentleman. It is just hard to get past that aloof exterior you show to most people."

Justin glared at his friend for a moment. "May I finish my story?"

"Please do. I'm all ears."

"As I was saying, after a few days had passed I decided to attempt to make conversation with her. I was aware of particular sensations overtaking my mind and body. I was forced to admit I had feelings of attraction for her. I determined the best way to rid myself of the silly emotions was to engage her in conversation. I was convinced she would be like all the other unmarried, pretty young women I have encountered. She would shy away at any subject I might bring up that would require clever, observant replies on her part. I would quickly lose interest and any sensation of enchantment I had for her would disappear."

"Enchantment? You were captivated by this woman!"

"I will admit, she set me back on my heels." Justin put a palm against his forehead and stared at the opposite wall for a moment before resuming his story. "To my surprise, I found her to be a very thoughtful, intelligent woman. We had several enjoyable, thought-provoking discussions together. After much deliberation, I decided to declare my interest. A situation arose immediately afterward that required quick action on my part to insure Miss Simms's well-being."

"I hope you were able to avert disaster from happening?"

"Yes I was. However in doing so, I found my arms wrapped around her and my face pressed close to her full, red lips. I remember they were trembling. I couldn't stop myself. I kissed her. Much to my astonishment, she rebuffed my advances and informed me that she was promised to marry another."

Robert moved over to Justin's side and laid a hand on his shoulder. "That is unfortunate, Justin. I'm very sorry if you were hurt by the experience. Don't allow that circumstance hold you back from meeting another special woman. Look at my Selina. You know how wonderful she is. It's entirely possible there is a lady somewhere who could bring you great joy and love."

"Selina, Lady Crestor is very special. You are fortunate to have her as your wife." He paused, frowning down at the carpet. "I never thought about it before, but perhaps you are right. I've guarded my heart, except in that one instance, because I've worried my future wife will be unfaithful and cause me great sadness as my mother did to my father."

A knock sounded upon the door.

"Enter."

Justin's butler Huxton pushed the door open and bowed with a flourish. "You have more visitors, my lord; Lady Greer, Miss Elizabeth Croft, Mrs. Wexley and Mr. John Wexley."

The three ladies entered the room first, with his cousin bringing up the rear. "Aunt Clara and John, welcome. This is my good friend, Robert, Lord Crestor. Introduce me to your betrothed, young man."

John reached for the hand of the pretty, diminutive blond lady standing next to him. "This is Miss Elizabeth Croft, daughter of Mr. Eliza Croft, a very successful jeweler in London."

She curtsied to him and then rose up to face him, blushing rosily. "It is an honor to meet you at last, Lord Rockton. John has told me much about you."

"I trust he has mentioned nothing but good things, Miss Croft." He smiled down at her and then turned toward the other woman, who he hadn't yet acknowledged. "Lady Greer, I believe? Are you a relation?"

The lady's head was bowed, her features hidden underneath her bonnet. She faced him now. "No, Lord Rockton, I am Miss Croft's companion."

"What the devil?" He gasped in shock. "Catherine? Miss Simms? Lady…?"

"Greer. Yes, my lord you have all the names and titles in correct succession." She took a deep breath and pursed her lips before continuing. "There is one other item of note. I was widowed a year and a half ago. The new heir to my late husband's title has not yet married, so I am also the Dowager Viscountess."

"I'm…I'm sorry. I didn't know." He stared at her features and noted worry lines around her eyes. She also seemed to have lost the sparkle and infectious enthusiasm that he had so admired when he had first met her. "I apologize for my language as well. You surprised me."

"Lady Greer. It is an honor to meet you." Robert stepped around him. "Your late husband served in my regiment. He spoke about you."

"Lord Crestor? You knew Colin? You must tell me all you remember of him."

Justin looked across the room, noting his aunt was deep in discussion with her son and Miss Croft. "I would know more of your story as well, Lady Greer. Shall I have my housekeeper show each of you to your rooms? You can settle in and then join us in the drawing room for tea in an hour."

"Yes, thank you. That would be best."

Justin walked across the room and yanked on the bell pull.

Huxton entered the room moments later. "Yes, my lord?"

"Have Mrs. Pulley show the ladies to their rooms, Huxton. Also, inform Cook we would like afternoon tea in an hour in the drawing room."

"Yes, my lord. Please follow me, my lady, Mrs. Wexler, and Miss Croft."

"I will go up and change as well," announced John as he followed the women out into the entry

As soon as the door closed behind him Robert spoke. "Is Lady Greer the woman you referred to earlier?"

Justin could not keep the surprise he felt from showing on his face. "However did you guess?"

Robert grinned at him. "Your reaction when you saw her clearly was priceless. I've never seen you respond to any other woman in such a way. I wouldn't have been surprised if you'd fallen prostrate to the floor."

"Nonsense, my feelings couldn't have been that transparent." As soon as he spoke, Justin realized he had done a poor job of hiding his emotional attachment to Catherine.

"Perhaps not, John is clearly smitten with Miss Croft and your aunt was busy admiring the two of them cooing together like love birds on the other side of the room. Lady Greer was probably expecting you to be startled by her appearance."

Justin sighed. "She has changed; much more somber and subdued, didn't laugh at all. She always made a tinkling, cheery sound when she laughed."

"Her life has altered substantially. She can't have been married long before she was widowed."

"Now she spends her days as a paid companion to motherless ladies? I am anxious to hear what she has to say about this turn of events. By the way, did the late Lord Greer often speak of her?"

Robert shrugged his shoulders. "I hope I didn't give

the impression he was forever prosing on about his wife. I can think of two instances that he made reference to her in my presence."

Justin frowned as he thought of what Catherine's reaction might have been to her husband's seemingly hasty departure. "Did he feel guilty about leaving her so soon after they were married?"

"No, I would describe his state of mind as relieved. He told me he had done his duty and married the woman he had been promised to in a long-standing agreement between their fathers. He also mentioned her the morning before his last battle. He said he was glad that she would always be taken care of if he should be killed."

A knock sounded, and Huxton entered the room. "My lord, Lady Crestor has arrived with Lord and Lady Burford. Another carriage follows with Lord and Lady Dunstable."

Robert moved to the open door. "It appears the rest of my family is here. I will see to their needs and meet you in the drawing room. I have a sense this Christmas is going to be an interesting one."

Justin was thwarted in his quest to seek an audience with Catherine when tea was served an hour later. The new arrivals were introduced once everyone had gathered in the room. She and Miss Croft were quickly monopolized by Selina, Lady Crestor as well as Selina's mother, Lady Burford. Aunt Clara and Robert's mother Lady Dunstable became engrossed in a discussion involving the benefits of rose water as a skin softener. The gentlemen were having an animated conversation on the use of dogs when hunting rabbits and gorse. They called him over to their group, eager for his opinion before he was able to have a word with Catherine.

Sometime later, when the teapots were dry and only crumbs remained on the plates that had been piled high with cucumber sandwiches and gingerbread, the ladies announced their intention to retire to their rooms to dress for dinner. Justin hastily excused himself from the lively debate he was participating in when he saw a chance to speak to his quarry.

"Catherine, Lady Greer, we must talk." He glanced at the others as they made their way to the door. "Alone."

She excused herself from Miss Croft's side and walked toward him with a melancholy expression. She sighed before she spoke. "In large gatherings such as this, it is very hard to do such a thing, my lord."

Justin wasn't about to adopt such a defeatist attitude. "I have a suggestion. My aunt informed me that a round of whist is to be played tonight after dinner. Although she never plays herself, she deems it an important pastime to be offered for the guests' amusement. Taking my aunt, as well as ourselves, out of the mix leaves eight people to play, making the numbers correct. We may retire to a corner of the room and have our discourse in relative privacy."

Her full lips twitched and then turned upward into a semblance of a smile. "It appears you have deliberated with much seriousness on this matter, my lord."

He grinned down at her, relieved to see a glimmer of her former, cheery disposition returning. "Challenging situations call for original solutions, my lady."

Her eyes twinkled as she smiled up at him, offering her hand. "You are nothing if not resourceful then. I look forward to our discussion, my lord."

He was conscious of a warm, comforting sensation in his chest. His heart felt as if it swelled with gladness when he saw the glimmer in her eyes.

"No more than I," he whispered as he bent over and clasped her gloved fingers in his own.

Chapter Five

"You must not doubt that your late husband felt great compassion for you." Lord Crestor pierced a chunk of goose meat with his fork.

Catherine had been given the seat next to him at dinner. Until this moment, his attention had been given to the other guests at the table. She took a sip of wine before answering. "I assure you, Lord Crestor, your statement does not surprise me. Colin always treated me with the utmost consideration and kindness during the brief time we were together as man and wife."

"Why do I detect a tone of sarcasm in your voice?"

"I have had many days since Colin's death to deliberate over the dizzying amount of change and adjustments to my life immediately before and after my marriage. I admit I was hurt when he left me so soon after the ceremony. We never ridiculed ourselves by saying that we loved each other, but I was certainly ready to spend the time to get to know him and perhaps one day feel a deep affection for him." She studied Lord Crestor's expression, hoping he understood the sincerity in her words.

"You are to be commended for your good intentions. I know a few couples who were forced to wed by their families. I believe little or no effort was made to form attachments. None of the unions were happy. They each live in separate residences. I hope your husband's desertion of you didn't cause you too much pain?" He nodded to a servant nearby, waiting to remove his empty plate.

Catherine waited to reply until her dish had also been taken away. "After much thought, I believe he was comforted by the knowledge that he had fulfilled our fathers' last requests with the additional appeasement that I would be well provided for in the event of his death. He was secure in this, and he was able to do what he wished with his life without feeling a sense of guilt."

"Although he was not with the regiment for very long before his death, I can tell you my impression of him with regard to yourself." Lord Crestor took another sip of his wine.

Catherine was conscious of a sense of trepidation as she heard his words. Once she had come to terms with Colin's hasty departure, she had assumed he hadn't spared a thought for her. "I would be grateful for the insight, my lord."

Lord Crestor turned in his seat so that he faced her. "During the two occasions he spoke of you to me, I also sensed that he was comforted and relieved to have done what was required of him when he married you. After following through on the betrothal agreement, he felt he was entitled to live his life the way he wished to. He told me that joining the cavalry gave him a sense of worth and importance that he didn't feel tucked away in the countryside on his estate. Perhaps he wasn't ready to be saddled with a wife. I hope I'm not being too harsh?"

Her anxiety had been for nothing it seemed. Colin had fulfilled the obligation and gone on to live his life his way without further concern for her. "No, your honesty is quite refreshing, my lord. I'm certain your guesses as to his motives are correct. In fairness, it should also be noted that I wasn't eager to be married, despite my advanced age of twenty-two."

"I would implore you, Lady Greer, not to take your initial, awkward, and unhappy experience with marriage as the standard outcome for all unions between a man and a woman." He cast a loving glance across the table at his wife. "I can attest that appreciation and as well as great love for one another at the start can bring one untold amounts of happiness and joy in life."

"I will remember what you have said, my lord," she answered before a query from Elizabeth took her attention elsewhere.

A short time later, when the plates had been cleared away and the wine glasses emptied, Lord Rockton stood up from his seat at the head of the table. "I would ask that the gentlemen forgo their cigars and brandy tonight. Game tables have been set up in the drawing room for whist. Please join me there as soon as you can."

Not long afterward, everyone had gathered inside the room. Mrs. Wexley sat on the seat of an overstuffed chair placed directly in front of the fireplace. Her son walked over and moved the embroidery frame she was working on closer to her side. The whist players divided themselves into two groups of four and took their seats.

"Do you have everything you need, Mother?"

"Yes, thank you. This is perfect, John. Enjoy your game."

Catherine stood to one side of the tables. Lord Rockton had yet to make an appearance.

"Are you certain you don't wish to play?" Lady Dunstable called out. "You're welcome to take my place."

"Lady Greer is going to keep me company." Lord Rockton was suddenly standing next to her, clasping her gloved hand and putting it on his arm. "Come over here. We will not be disturbed."

He led her to an L-shaped window seat on the far side of the room. Heavy, crimson velvet drapes were drawn against the chilly temperature outside.

"Thank you, my lord." Catherine sat on one cushion and Lord Rockton took the other.

"Are you warm enough? We could move closer to the fire if you wish."

"This is perfectly fine."

"Good." His gaze moved over her face. "First, I wish to inquire, Catherine, how you came to be a hired companion."

"My lord…"

"Justin, please."

"Very well, Justin. I must explain something about myself. I need to feel useful to be happy. I was excited to begin my life as a married lady. I imagined all the ways I would be needed; my husband would want my companionship, the housekeeper would look to me for advice and suggestions on running my new home, Cook would want to hear my meal preferences, and the gardeners would inquire about the names of my favorite flowers." She smiled at him, hoping she didn't sound foolish.

He grinned at her. "You started with the best intentions to be a good wife to him."

"Instead, less than three months after I arrived at Greer Estate as a new bride, I learned I was a widow and I moved to the Dower House. During the following year of mourning, I lived there quietly with only Miss Wicker and my maid for company."

"Your life has undergone great change in a very short period of time. How is Miss Wicker?"

"She passed away suddenly last summer."

Justin put his hand on her arm. "I'm very sorry to hear that."

"Thank you. I do miss her."

"You have been living alone in the Dower House since that time? Do you have visitors?"

She sighed before speaking. "Occasionally a footman or a maid is sent over from the main house to check on me. Generally, the only contact I have with others is through my personal maid and my cook. However, soon after my mourning period was finished, Mary wrote inviting me to join her and her family at their townhouse in London. I was very grateful for the invitation. I longed to be part of the bustling metropolis once again."

"I can imagine Edward and Mary were both concerned for your well-being."

"Yes, they were. But I fear I gave Mary palpitations when I arrived on her doorstep. I hadn't been eating or sleeping well for some time."

He frowned down at her with a worried expression on his face. "I trust you were quickly put to rights under their care?"

"I soon became fit once again. It was wonderful to be part of a loving, happy family. The days were busy ones. We went shopping together, took walks, and fed the ducks at the park."

Justin studied her intently. "I'm very glad to hear you didn't languish away inside your room while you were there."

"Although I didn't attend any evening parties during my visit, Mary invited a few other ladies with children who were staying in town for the summer over to tea. It was during this event that it was mentioned the wealthy, influential jeweler, Mr. Eliza Croft was interested in obtaining a titled lady or widow as a companion for his daughter. I knew this was something I would enjoy doing. It would give me a chance to be of use to someone even if they were of the merchant class. It doesn't bother you my lo…Justin that Elizabeth is one of them?" She barely breathed, staring at him, waiting for his answer.

"Not in the least. The important thing is that John and Elizabeth are deeply in love; the passion and affection they feel now for each other will continue to grow and last for an eternity." He stopped speaking and glanced over at the game tables where many teasing comments and laughter could be heard. "I sense they have those emotions. I am very happy that they discovered each other."

Catherine's breath hitched in her throat as she listened to his impassioned speech. "It's…It's wonderful to hear you are capable of expressing such things."

"You are referring once again to my legendary, callous attitude to love and marriage?" He shrugged his broad shoulders and let out a sigh. "Robert, Lord Crestor has brought to my attention that my own avoidance of those subjects could possibly stem from my late mother's insensitive treatment of my father soon after I was born until her death eight years ago."

Catherine was surprised to hear this of his mother. "How was she insensitive?"

"She spent little time at home after recovering from

my difficult birth and was quite legendary for the large number of lovers she had after that event. I now realize her actions could have made me hesitant to offer my heart to a lady believing it would be trampled upon immediately after she produced my heir." He became quiet and looked down at his hands.

Catherine was suddenly conscious of a painful ache in her chest. A sensation of great sadness threatened to overwhelm her. "My lord...Justin, surely you can't think all women are so cold-hearted?"

His green eyes appeared to darken as he stared at her face. "No, no I don't. Not any longer."

She felt great relief as he said those words. "I...I wanted to tell you. I...I never quite forgot you after we said good-bye to each other two years ago. I know it was simply a momentary attraction for us both. The joyous spirit of Christmas was upon us, combined with interesting conversations around the fire, the warmth and comfort of delicious meals paired with excellent wine. But those memories have provided me with a sense of tenderness and pleasure when I needed them most."

"A momentary attraction? Is that what you believe?" He reached for her hand and placed it upon his sleeve once more. "Come, I wish to speak to you in private."

Catherine raised her eyebrows in surprise but stood and followed him across the room to the door.

Mrs. Wexley looked up from her embroidery frame. "Is everything all right, Justin?"

"Yes, yes, Aunt. I simply need to clear up a matter of confusion."

He opened the door, gesturing for Catherine to

precede him. She stepped out into the hallway with Justin following closely behind.

"May I do something for you, my lord?" the butler inquired from his post near the front entry.

"Make yourself scarce for a time, will you, Huxton?"

"Yes, of course, my lord."

"We can be as secluded as possible in here under the circumstances." Justin led her across the hall to an alcove. He turned her to face him and clasped both her hands in his own. "I want to make certain that you understand what I'm saying, Catherine. There is another reason why I never found a woman I could love. Can you imagine how it feels to have young ladies barely out of the schoolroom, paraded in front of you with false smiles on their faces; having no interest in the person you are other than the fact that you are a titled, wealthy peer with a large, prosperous estate?"

"Have you forgotten my previous circumstances? I would never condone a loveless marriage."

He moved closer. "You do understand me then. I wish…"

"You…you wish me well." Her voice shook. She looked at the floor not wanting to see what she what she was certain would be only friendly affection reflected in his eyes. She became aware of his muscular thigh pressing against her leg. She forced herself to continue. "That is what you said the last time we parted."

"No! I never want you to leave me!" He pulled her closer and rested his chin on the crown of her head. "When you walked into my life two years ago, a fresh, eager, lovely face full of happiness, intelligence and natural gaiety, I felt thankfulness and humility in your presence. It was wonderful to see a woman who was truly happy and comfortable in a world of her own making."

"Thank you for saying such lovely things about me. I have to confess I haven't been that lady for many, many months."

He stepped away, reaching for her hands. His green eyes seemed to glow as he looked down at her. "You were promised to a man you barely knew. He left you soon after your marriage. Those are not circumstances to bring any woman comfort or happiness. Please tell me that the closeness we experienced together was something as special to you as it was to me."

She was silent a moment as she thought of the many unforgettable moments they had shared two years ago. "There was something very wonderful about those days."

"I was hoping you would say that." He tugged on her hands, pulling her closer. "I wish…I wish for you kiss, Catherine. Please, will you marry me? I love you so much."

Catherine looked up at him, seeking to memorize this moment while at the same time, savoring the sensations of joyousness and delight that swept into her heart as she heard his words. She was suddenly reminded of Lord Crestor's advice; not to give up on finding a special man to welcome into her life. Perhaps fate had dealt her a hand at a chance for true love. She laughed, the tinkling sounds of happiness had returned. "Should I answer the question first, my lord?"

He didn't reply. He gazed down at her with what she fancied was a special, intense look reserved only for her.

She pretended to ponder her answer a few moments more until she realized he was holding his breath. "I believe my reply is best given by granting your wish."

She reached up to clasp his neck with one hand, tugging gently on the leather strap that held his hair. She guided his head down until his lips met her own quivering ones. The instant their mouths touched, Catherine was spellbound. She was conscious of nothing else except for the wonder and awe of being held in Justin's arms and kissed by him.

Justin cupped her chin with his hand, their lips clung together a moment longer. Then he slowly raised his head, wrapped his arms around her shoulders and held her close. "You have given me all I desire with that embrace. The promise of you, by my side forever as my wife; it's almost like a dream."

She smiled up at him through her tears. "Believe it is real. I look forward to making many wonderful memories with you."

"You're crying. What is wrong?"

"Nothing at all. I'm so grateful to have you."

He bent and kissed her cheek. "No one could be more thankful than I, my darling. It took some time to happen, but we were meant to be together."

A word about the author...

I am a native Southern Californian. When I was very young, I discovered my local library and the exciting potential of escaping the real world inside the pages of a good book. As a teenager, I became a huge fan of British literature. After reading most of the Victorian classics, I came upon Regency period novels in 1987. It was love at first read. Since my chance introduction to this wonderful era in time, I have read over three thousand fiction novels, and I own a large collection of research books on the period.

www.ingramcontent.com/pod-product-compliance
Lightning Source LLC
Chambersburg PA
CBHW070924180626
46817CB00003B/1186